"The only thing I know is that you are a stubborn and defiant woman who has tested me beyond endurance," he said, his voice rough. **"And maybe this has been inevitable all along."**

She stared into his eyes. "You're going to put me across your lap and smack my bottom?"

"Is that what you'd like? Maybe later. But not right now. Right now I'm going to kiss you—but be warned that this is going to spoil you for anyone else. Are you prepared for that, Amber? That every man who kisses you after this is going to make you remember me and ache for me?"

"You are *so* arrogant," she accused.

But her lips were parting and Conall knew she wanted this just as much as him. Maybe more—for he caught a flash of hunger in her darkening eyes. Sliding one hand around her waist while the other cushioned her still-damp hair, he lowered his mouth to hers.

Wedlocked!

Conveniently wedded, passionately bedded!

Whether there's a debt to be paid, a will to be obeyed or a business to be saved...

She's got no choice but to say, "I do!"

But these billionaire bridegrooms have got another think coming if they imagine the marriage will be that easy...

Soon their convenient brides become the objects of *inconvenient* desires!

Find out what happens after the vows in

Untouched Until Marriage
by Chantelle Shaw

The Billionaire's Defiant Acquisition
by Sharon Kendrick

One Night to Wedding Vows
by Kim Lawrence

Look for more stories coming soon!

Sharon Kendrick

THE BILLIONAIRE'S DEFIANT ACQUISITION

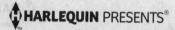

HARLEQUIN PRESENTS®

Recycling programs
for this product may
not exist in your area.

ISBN-13: 978-0-373-13901-9

The Billionaire's Defiant Acquisition

First North American Publication 2016

Copyright © 2016 by Sharon Kendrick

Printed in U.S.A.

www.Harlequin.com

Sharon Kendrick once won a national writing competition by describing her ideal date: being flown to an exotic island by a gorgeous and powerful man. Little did she realize that she'd just wandered into her dream job! Today she writes for Harlequin, featuring her often stubborn but always *to-die-for* heroes and the women who bring them to their knees. She believes that the best books are those you never want to end. Just like life...

Books by Sharon Kendrick

Harlequin Presents

The Ruthless Greek's Return
Christmas in Da Conti's Bed
The Greek's Marriage Bargain
A Scandal, a Secret, a Baby
The Sheikh's Undoing
Monarch of the Sands
Too Proud to Be Bought

The Bond of Billionaires

Claimed for Makarov's Baby
The Sheikh's Christmas Conquest

One Night With Consequences

Carrying the Greek's Heir

At His Service

The Housekeeper's Awakening

Desert Men of Qurhah

Defiant in the Desert
Shamed in the Sands
Seduced by the Sultan

With special thanks to fascinating Fredrik Ferrier,
for giving me an illuminating glimpse into
the world of art.

And to the fabulous Annie Macdonald Hall—
who taught me so much about horses—and made
me understand why people love them so much.

CHAPTER ONE

IN THE FLESH she looked more dangerous than beautiful. Conall's mouth hardened. She was exquisite, yes…but *faded*. Like a rose which had been plucked fresh for a man's buttonhole before a wild night of partying, but which now lay wilted and drooping across his chest.

Fast asleep, she lay sprawled on top of a white leather sofa. She was wearing a baggy T-shirt, which curved over her breasts and bottom, ending midway along amazingly tanned legs which seemed to go on for ever. Beside her lay an empty champagne glass—the finger-marked crystal upended and glinting in the spring sunshine. A faint breeze drifted in from the open windows leading onto the balcony, but it wasn't enough to disperse the faint fug of cigarette smoke, along with the musky scent of incense. Conall made a barely perceptible click of distaste. Cliché after cliché were all here—embodied in the magnificent body of Amber Carter as she lay with her head pillowed on her arm and her black hair spilling like ink over her golden skin.

If she'd been a man he would have shaken her awake with a contemptuous hand, but she was not a man. She was a woman. A spoilt and distractingly beautiful woman who was now his responsibility and for some reason he didn't want to touch her. He didn't dare.

Damn Ambrose Carter, he thought viciously, remembering the older man's plaintive appeal to him. *You've got to save her from herself, Conall. Someone has to show her she can't carry on like this.* And damn his own stupid conscience, which had made him agree to carry out this crazy deal.

He listened. The apartment was silent—but maybe he should check it was empty. That there were no other bodies sprawled in one of the many bedrooms and able to hear what he was about to say to her.

He prowled from room to room, but, among all the debris of cold pizza lying in greasy boxes and half-empty bottles of vintage champagne, he could find no one. Only once did he pause—when he pushed open a door of a spare bedroom, cluttered with books and clothes and a dusty-looking exercise bike. Half hidden behind a velvet sofa was a stack of paintings and Conall walked over to them, his natural collector's eye making him flick through them with interest. The canvases were raw and angry—with swirls and splodges of paint, some of which had been highlighted with a sharp edging of black ink. He studied them for several moments, until he was forced to remember that he was here for a purpose and he turned away from the pictures and returned to the sitting room, to find Amber Carter lying exactly where he'd left her.

'Wake up,' he growled. And then, when that received no response, he repeated it—more loudly this time. 'I said, wake up.'

She moved. A golden arm reached up to brush aside the thick sweep of ebony hair which obscured most of her face, offering him a sudden unimpeded view of her profile. Her cute little nose and the natural pout of her rosy lips. Thick lashes fluttered open and as she slowly turned her head to look at him he realised that her eyes were the most startling shade of green he'd ever seen. They made the breath dry in his throat, those eyes. They made him momentarily forget what he was doing there.

'What's going on?' she questioned, in a smoky voice. 'And who the hell are you?'

She sat up, blinking as she looked around— but not creating the kind of fuss he might have expected. As if she was used to being woken by strange men who had walked into her apartment at midday. He felt another shimmer of distaste. Maybe she was.

'My name is Conall Devlin,' he said, looking at her face for some kind of recognition, but seeing only a blank and shuttered boredom on her frozen features.

'Oh, yeah?' Those amazing eyes swept over him and then she yawned. 'And how did you get in, Conall Devlin?'

In many ways Conall was the most old-fashioned of men—an accusation levelled at him many times by disappointed women in the past—and in that precise moment he felt his temper begin to flare because it confirmed everything he'd heard about her. That she was careless. That she didn't care about anything or anyone, except herself. And anger was safer than desire. Than allowing himself to focus on the way her breasts jiggled as she moved.

Or to acknowledge that as she rose to her feet and walked across the room she moved with a natural grace, which made him want to stare at her and keep staring. Which made his groin begin to harden with an unwilling kind of lust.

'The door was open,' he said, not bothering to hide his disapproval.

'Oh. Right. Someone must have left it open on their way out.' She looked at him and smiled the pretty kind of smile which probably had most men eating out of her hand. 'I had a party last night.'

He didn't smile back. 'Doesn't it worry you that someone could have walked right in and burgled you—or worse?'

She shrugged. 'Not really. Security on the main door is usually very tight. Though come to think of it—you seem to have got past them without too much difficulty. How did you manage that?'

'Because I have a key,' he said, holding it up between his thumb and forefinger so that it glinted in the bright spring sunshine.

She was walking across the room—the baggy T-shirt moving across her bottom to draw his unwilling attention to the pert swell of her buttocks. But his words made her jerk her head back in surprise and a faint frown appeared on her brow as she extracted a pack of cigarettes from a small beaded handbag which was lying on a coffee table.

'What are you talking about, you *have a key*?' she questioned, pulling out a filter tip and jamming it in between her lips.

'I'd rather you didn't light that,' said Conall tightly.

Her eyes narrowed. 'Oh, really?'

'Yes. *Really*,' he gritted back sarcastically. 'Discounting the obvious dangers of passive smoking, I happen to hate the smell.'

'Then leave. Nobody's stopping you.' She flicked the lighter with a manicured thumbnail so that a blue-gold flash of flame flared briefly into life, but she only got as far as inhaling the first drag when Conall crossed the room and removed the cigarette from her mouth, ignoring her look of shock.

'What the hell do you think you're playing at?' she spluttered indignantly. 'You can't do that!'

'No?' he questioned silkily. 'Watch me, baby.' He walked out to the balcony and crushed the glowing red tip between thumb and forefinger, before dropping it into another empty champagne glass, which was standing next to a large pot plant.

When he returned he could see a look of defiance on her face as she took out a second cigarette.

'There are plenty more where that came from,' she taunted.

'And you'll only be wasting your time,' he said flatly. 'Because every cigarette you light I'm going to take from you and extinguish, until eventually you have none left.'

'And if I call the police and have you arrested for trespass and harassment,' she challenged. 'What then?'

Conall shook his head. 'Sorry to disappoint you, but neither of those charges will stand up—since I think the law might find that you are the one who is actually guilty of trespass. Remember what I just told you? That I have a key.' He paused.

He saw her defiance briefly waver. He saw a shadow cross over her beautiful green eyes and he felt a wave of something which felt almost like empathy and he wasn't quite sure why. Until he reminded himself what kind of woman she was. The spoilt, manipulative kind who stood for everything he most despised.

'Yes I know but I'm asking why—and it had better be a good explanation,' she said in a tone of voice which nobody had dared use with him for years. 'Who are you, and why have you come barging in here, trying to take control?'

'I'm happy to tell you anything you want to know,' he said evenly. 'But first I think you need to put on some clothes.'

'Why?' A smile played at the corners of her lips as she put a hand on one angled hip and struck a catwalk pose. 'Does my appearance bother you, Mr Devlin?'

'Actually, no—at least, not in the way I think you're suggesting. I'm not turned on by women who smoke and flaunt their bodies to strangers,' he said, although the latter part of this statement wasn't quite true, as the continued aching in his body testified. He swallowed against the sudden unwanted dryness in his throat. 'And since I don't have all day to waste—why don't you do as I ask and then we can get down to business?'

For a moment Amber hesitated, tempted to tell him to go to hell. To carry through her threat and march over to the phone and call the police, despite the fact that she was enjoying the unexpected *drama* of the situation. Because wasn't it good to feel *something*—even if it was only anger, when for so long now all she had felt had been a terrifying kind of *numbness*? As if she were no longer made of flesh and blood, but was colourless and invisible—like water.

She narrowed her eyes as her mind flicked back through the previous evening. Had Conall Devlin been one of the many gate-crashers at the impromptu party she'd ended up hosting? No. Definitely not. She frowned. She would have remembered him. Definitely. Because he was the kind of man you would never forget, no matter how objectionable you found him.

Unwillingly, her gaze drifted over him. His rugged features would have been perfect were it not for the fact that his nose had obviously once been broken. His hair was dark—though not quite as dark as hers—and his eyes were the colour of midnight. His jaw was dark and shadowed—as if he hadn't bothered shaving that morning, as if he had more than his fair share of testosterone raging around his body. And what a body. Amber swallowed. He looked as if he would be perfectly at ease smashing a pickaxe into a tough piece of concrete—even though she could tell that his immaculate charcoal suit must have cost a fortune.

And meanwhile the inside of her mouth felt as if it had been turned into sandpaper and she was certain her breath must smell awful because she'd fallen asleep without brushing her teeth. Her fingers crept up surreptitiously to her face. Yesterday's make-up was still clogging her eyes and beneath the baggy T-shirt her skin felt warm and sticky. It wasn't how you wanted to look when you were presented with a man as spectacular as him.

'Okay,' she said carelessly. 'I'll go and get dressed.'

She enjoyed his brief look of surprise—as if he hadn't been expecting her sudden capitulation—and that pleased her because she liked surprising people. She could feel his gaze on her as she padded out of the room towards her bedroom, which had a breathtaking view over some of London's most famous landmarks.

She stared at the perfect circle of the London Eye as she tried to gather her thoughts together. Some women might have been freaked out at having been woken in such a way by a total stranger, but all Amber could think was that it made an interesting start to the day, when lately her days all seemed to bleed into one meaningless blur. She wondered if *Conall Devlin* was used to getting everything he wanted. Probably. He had that unmistakable air of arrogance about him. Did he think she would be intimidated by his macho stance and bossy air? Well, he would soon realise that nothing intimidated *her*.

Nothing.

She didn't rush to get ready—although she took the precaution of locking the bathroom door first. A power shower woke her into life and after she'd dressed, she carefully applied her make-up. A quick blast of the hairdryer and she was done. Twenty minutes later she emerged in a pair of skinny jeans and a clingy white T-shirt to find him still there. Just not where she'd left him—dominating the large reception room with that faintly hostile glint in his midnight-blue eyes. Instead, he was sitting on one of the sofas, busy tapping something into a laptop, as if he had every right to make himself at home. He glanced up as she walked in and she saw a look in his eyes which made her feel faintly uncomfortable, before he closed the laptop and surveyed her coolly.

'Sit down,' he said.

'This is my home, not yours and therefore you don't start telling me what to do. I don't want to sit down.'

'I think it's better you do.'

'I don't care what you think.'

His eyes narrowed. 'You don't care about very much at all, do you, Amber?'

Amber stiffened. He said her name as if he had every right to. As if it were something he'd been rehearsing. And now she could make out the faint Irish burr in his deep voice. Her heart lurched because suddenly this had stopped feeling like a whacky alternative to a normal Sunday morning—whatever *normal* was— and had begun to feel rather…disturbing.

But she sat down on the sofa opposite his, because standing in front of him was making her feel like a naughty schoolgirl who had been summoned in front of the headmaster. And something about the way he was looking at her was making her knees wobble in a way which had nothing to do with anger.

She stared at him. 'Just who are you?'

'I told you. Conall Devlin.' He smiled. 'Name still not ringing any bells?'

She shrugged, as something drifted faintly into the distant recesses of her mind and then drifted out again. 'Maybe.'

'I know your brother, Rafe—'

'*Half*-brother,' she corrected with cold emphasis. 'I haven't seen Rafe in years. He lives in Australia.' She gave a brittle smile. 'We're a very fragmented family.'

'So I believe. I also used to work for your father.'

'My father?' She frowned. 'Oh, dear. Poor you.'

The look which greeted this remark showed that she'd irritated him and for some reason this pleased her. Amber reminded herself that he had no right to storm in and sit on one of her sofas, uninvited. Or to sit there barking out questions. The trouble was that he was exuding a disturbing air of confidence and certainty—like a magician who was saving his show-stopping trick right for the end of his act…

'Anyway,' she said, with an entirely unnecessary glance at the diamond watch which was glittering furiously at her wrist. 'I really don't have time for all this. I'll admit it was a novel way to be woken up but I'm getting bored now and I'm meeting friends for lunch. So cut to the chase and tell me why you're here, Mr Conall. Is my dear daddy having one of his occasional bouts of remorse and wondering how his children are getting on? Are you one of his heavies who he's sent to find out how I am? In which case, you can tell him I'm doing just fine.' She raised her eyebrows at him. 'Or has he grown bored with wife number...let me see, which number is he on now? Is it six? Or has he reached double figures? It's *so-o-o* difficult to keep up with his hectic love life.'

Conall listened as she spat out her spiky observations, telling himself that of *course* she was likely to be mixed up and angry and combative. That anyone with her troubled background was never going to end up taking the conventional path in life. Except he knew that adversity didn't necessarily have to make you spoilt and petulant. He thought about what his own mother had been forced to endure—the kind of hardship which would probably be beyond Amber Carter's wilful understanding.

His mouth tightened. He wouldn't be doing her any favours by patting her on her pretty, glossy head and telling her it was all going to be okay. Hadn't people been doing that all her life—with predictable results? Quite frankly, he was itching to lay her across his lap and spank a little sense into her. He felt an unwanted jerk of lust. Though maybe that wasn't such a good idea.

'I have just concluded a business deal with your father,' he said.

'Bully for you,' she said flippantly. 'No doubt he drove a hard bargain.'

'Indeed he did,' he agreed steadily, wondering if she had any idea of the irony of her words—and how much he secretly agreed with them. Because if anyone else had attempted to negotiate the kind of terms Ambrose Carter had demanded, then Conall would have given an emphatic no and walked away from the deal without looking back. But the acquisition of this imposing tower block in this part of London wasn't just something he'd set his heart on—a lifetime dream he'd never thought he'd achieve just shy of his thirty-fifth birthday. It was more than that. He owed the old man. He owed him big time. Because despite Ambrose's own car crash of an emotional life, he had shown Conall kindness at a time when his life had been short of kindness. He had given him the break he'd needed. Had believed in him when nobody else had.

'You owe me, Conall,' he'd said as he had outlined his outrageous demand. 'Do this one thing for me and we're quits.'

And even though Conall had inwardly objected to the blatant emotional blackmail, how could he possibly have refused? If it weren't for Ambrose he could have ended up serving time in prison. His life could have been very different. Surely it wasn't beyond the realms of possibility that he could teach his mixed-up daughter a few fundamental lessons in manners and survival.

He stared into her emerald eyes and tried to ignore the sensual curve of her mouth, which was sending subliminal messages to his body and making a pulse at his temple begin to hammer. 'Yesterday, I made a significant purchase from your father.'

She wasn't really paying attention. She was too busy casting longing looks in the direction of her cigarettes. 'And your point is?'

'My point is that I now own this apartment block,' he said.

He had her attention now. All of it. Her

green eyes were shocked—she looked like a cat which had had a bucket of icy water thrown over it. But it didn't take longer than a couple of seconds for her natural arrogance to assert itself. For her to narrow those amazing eyes and look down her haughty little nose at him.

'You? But…but it's been in his property portfolio for years. It's one of his key investments. Why would he sell it without telling me?' She wrinkled her brow in confusion. 'And to you?'

Conall gave a short laugh. The inference was as clear as the blue spring sky outside the penthouse windows. He wondered if she would have found the news less shocking if the purchase had been made by some rich aristocrat—someone who presumably she would have less trouble twisting around her little finger.

'Presumably because he likes doing business with me,' he said. 'And he wants to free up some of his money and commitments in order to enjoy his retirement.'

Another frown pleated her perfect brow. 'I had no idea he was thinking about retirement.'

Conall was tempted to suggest that if she communicated with her father a little more often, then she might know what was going on in his life, but he wasn't here to judge her. He was here to offer her a solution to her current appalling lifestyle, even if it went against his every instinct.

'Well, he is. He's winding down and as of now I am the new owner of this development.' He drew in a deep breath. 'Which means, of course, that there are going to be a number of changes. The main one being that you can no longer continue to live here rent-free as you have been doing.'

'Excuse me?'

'You are currently occupying a luxury apartment in a prime location,' he continued, 'which I can rent out for an astronomical monthly sum. At the moment you are paying precisely nothing and I'm afraid that the arrangement is about to come to an end.'

Her haughty expression became even haughtier and she shuddered, as if the very mention of money was in some way vulgar, and Conall felt a flicker of pleasure as he realised he was enjoying himself. Because it was a long time since a woman had shown him anything except an eager green light.

'I don't think you understand, Mr... *Dev-*

lin,' she continued, spitting his name out as if it were poison, 'that you will get your money. I'm quite happy to pay the current market value as rent. I just need to speak to my bank,' she concluded.

He gave a smile. 'Good luck with that.'

She was getting angry now. He could see it in the sudden glitter of her eyes and the way she curled her scarlet fingernails so that they looked like talons against the faded denim of her skinny jeans. And he felt a corresponding flicker of something he didn't recognise. Something he tried to push away as he stared into the furious tremble of her lips.

'You may know my father and my brother,' she said, 'but that certainly doesn't give you the authority to make pronouncements about things which are none of your business. Things about which you know nothing. Like my finances.'

'Oh, I know more about those than you might realise,' he said. 'More than you would probably be comfortable with.'

'I don't believe you.'

'Believe what you like, baby,' he said softly. 'Because you'll soon find out what's true. But it doesn't have to get acrimonious. I'm going to be very magnanimous, Amber, because your father and I go back a long way. And I'm going to make you an offer.'

Her magnificent eyes narrowed suspiciously. 'What kind of offer?'

'I'm going to offer you a job and the chance to redeem yourself. And if you accept, we'll see about giving you an apartment more suited to a woman on a working wage, rather than this—' He gave an expansive wave of his hand. 'Which you have to admit is more suited to someone on a millionaire's salary.'

She was staring at him incredulously, as if she couldn't believe what he'd just said. As if he were suddenly going to smile and tell her that he'd simply been teasing and she could have whatever it was she wanted. Was that how men usually behaved towards her? he wondered. Of course it was. When you looked the way she looked, men would fall over themselves whenever she clicked her beautifully manicured fingers.

'And if I don't accept?'

He shrugged. 'That will make things a little more difficult. I will be forced to give you a month's notice and after that to change the locks, and I'm afraid you'll be on your own.'

She jumped to her feet, her eyes spitting green fire—looking as if she'd like to rush across the room and rake those scarlet talons all over him. And wasn't there a primitive side of him which wished she would go right ahead? Take them right down his chest to his groin. Curve those red nails around his balls and gently scrape them, before replacing them with the lick of her tongue.

But she didn't. She just stood there sucking in a deep breath and trying to compose herself…while his erotic little fantasies meant that he was having to do exactly the same.

'I may not know much about the law, Mr Devlin,' she said, biting out the words like splinters of ice, 'but even I know that you aren't allowed to throw a sitting tenant out onto the streets.'

'But you're not a tenant, Amber, and you never have been,' he said, trying not to show the sudden triumph which rushed through him. Because although she might be spoilt and thoroughly objectionable, she was going to learn enough of life's harsher lessons in the coming weeks, without him rubbing salt into the wound. He picked his next words carefully. 'Your father has been letting you live here as a favour, nothing more. You didn't sign any agreements—'

'Of course I didn't—because he's my *father*!'

'Which means that your occupancy was simply an act of kindness. And now he has sold it to me, I'm afraid he no longer has any interest or claims on the property. And as a consequence, neither do you.'

Wildly, she shook her head and ebony tendrils of hair flew around it. 'He wouldn't just have sprung it on me like this! He would have told me!' she said, her voice rising.

'He said he'd sent you a letter to inform you what was happening, and so had the bank.'

Amber shot an anguished glance over at the pile of mail which lay unopened on the desk. She had a terrible habit of putting letters to one side and ignoring them. She'd done it for longer than she could remember. Letters only ever contained bad news and all her bills were paid by direct debit and if people wanted her that badly, they could always send an email. Because that was what people did, wasn't it?

But in the meantime, she wasn't going to take any notice of this shadowed-jawed man with the mocking voice and a presence which was strangely unsettling. All she had to do was to speak to her father. There had to be some kind of mistake. There *had to*. Either that, or Daddy's brain wasn't as sharp as it had once been. Why else would he choose to sell one of the jewels in his property crown to this…this *thug*?

'I'd like you to leave now, Mr Devlin.'

He raised dark and mocking brows. 'So you're not interested in my offer? A proper job for the first time in your privileged life? The chance to show the world that you're more than just a vapid socialite who flits from party to party?'

'I'd sooner work for the devil than work for you,' she retorted, watching as he rose from the sofa and moved across the room until he was towering over her, with a grim expression on his dark face.

'Make an appointment to see me when you're ready to see sense,' he said, putting a business card down on the coffee table.

'That just isn't going to happen—be very sure about that,' she said, pulling a cigarette from the pack and glaring at him defiantly, as if daring him to stop her again. 'Now go to hell, will you?'

'Oh, believe me, baby,' he said softly. 'Hell would be a preferable alternative to a minute more spent in *your* company.'

And didn't it only add outrage to Amber's growing sense of panic to realise that he actually *meant* it?

CHAPTER TWO

AMBER'S FINGERS WERE trembling as she left the bank and little rivulets of sweat were trickling down over her hot cheeks. Impatiently brushing them aside, she stood stock-still outside the gleaming building while all around her busy City types made little tutting noises of irritation as they were forced to weave their way around her.

There had to be some kind of mistake. There had to be. She couldn't believe that her father would be so cruel. Or so dictatorial. That he would have instructed that tight-lipped bank manager to inform her that all funds in her account had been frozen, and no more would be forthcoming. But her rather hysterical request that the bank manager stop *freaking her out* had been met with nothing but an ominous silence and now that she was outside, the truth hit her like a sledgehammer coming at her out of nowhere.

She was broke.

Her heart slammed against her ribcage. Part of her still didn't want to believe it. Had the bank manager been secretly laughing at her when he'd handed over the formal-looking letter? She'd ripped it open and stared in horror as the words written by her father's lawyer had wobbled before her eyes and a key phrase had jumped out at her, like a spectre.

Conall Devlin has been instructed to provide any assistance you may need.

Conall Devlin? She had literally *shaken* with rage. Conall Devlin, the brute who had stormed into her apartment yesterday and who was responsible for her current state of homelessness? She would sooner starve than ask *him* for assistance. She would talk her father round and he would listen to her. He always did.

But in the middle of her defiance came an overwhelming wave of panic and fear, which washed over her and made her feel as if she were drowning. It was the same feeling she used to get when her mother would suddenly announce that they were leaving a city, and all

Amber's hard-fought-for friends would soon become distant and then forgotten memories.

She mustn't panic. She mustn't.

Her fingers still shaking, Amber sheltered in a shop doorway and took out her cell phone. She rang her father's number, but it went straight through to his personal assistant, Mary-Ellen, a woman who had never been her biggest fan and who didn't bother hiding her disapproval when she heard Amber's voice.

'Amber. This *is* a surprise,' she said archly.

'Hello, Mary-Ellen.' Amber drew in a deep breath. 'I need to speak to my father—urgently. Is he there?'

'I'm afraid he's not.'

'Do you know when he'll be back or where I can get hold of him?'

There was a pause and Amber wondered if she was being paranoid, or whether it sounded like a very deliberate pause.

'I'm afraid it isn't quite as easy as that. He's gone to an ashram in India.'

Amber gave a snort of disbelief and a passing businessman shot her a funny look. 'My father? Gone to an ashram? To do yoga and eat vegan food? Is this some kind of joke, Mary-Ellen?'

'No, it is not a joke,' said Mary-Ellen crisply. 'He's been trying to get hold of you for weeks. He's left a lawyer's letter with the bank—did you get it?'

Amber thought about the screwed-up piece of paper currently reposing with several sticks of chewing gum and various lipsticks at the bottom of her handbag. 'Yes, I got it.'

'Then I suggest you follow his advice and speak to Conall Devlin. All his contact details are there. Conall is the man who'll be able to help you in your father's absence. He's—'

With a howl of rage, Amber cut the connection and slung her phone back into her bag, before starting to walk—not knowing nor caring which direction she was taking. She didn't want *Conall Devlin* to help her! What was it with him that suddenly his name was on everyone's lips as if he were some kind of god? And what was it with her that she was behaving like some kind of helpless *victim*, just because a few obstacles had been put in her way?

Worse things than this had happened to her, she reminded herself. She'd survived a nightmare childhood, hadn't she? And even when she'd got through that, the problems hadn't stopped coming. She wiped a trickle of sweat away from her forehead. But those kinds of thoughts wouldn't help her now. She needed to think clearly. She needed to go back to the apartment to work out some kind of coping strategy until she could get hold of her father. And she *would* get hold of him. Somehow she would track him down—even if she had to hitchhike to the wretched ashram in order to do so. She would appeal to his better judgement and the sense of guilt which had never quite left him for kicking her and her mother out onto the street. Surely he wasn't planning to do that for a second time? And surely he hadn't *really* frozen her funds? But in the meantime…

She caught the Tube and got out near her apartment, stopping off at the nearest shop to buy some provisions since her rumbling stomach was reminding her that she'd had nothing to eat that morning. But after putting a whole stack of shopping and a pack of cigarettes through the till, she had the humiliation of seeing the machine decline her card. There was an audible sigh of irritation from the man in the queue behind her and she saw one woman nudging her friend as they moved closer as if anticipating some sort of scene.

'There must be some kind of mistake,' Amber mumbled, her face growing scarlet. 'I shop in here all the time—you must remember me? I can bring the money along later.'

But as the embarrassed shop assistant shook her head, she told Amber that it was company policy never to accept credit. And as she rang the bell underneath her till deep down Amber knew there had been no mistake. Her father really had done it. He'd *frozen her funds* just as the bank manager had told her.

She thought about her refrigerator at home and its meagre contents. There was plenty of champagne but little else—a tub of Greek yoghurt, which was probably growing a forest of mould by now, a bag of oranges and those soggy chocolate biscuits which were past their sell-by date. Her cheeks growing even hotter, Amber scrabbled around in her purse for some spare change and found nothing but a solitary, crumpled note.

'I'll just take the cigarettes,' she croaked, handing over the note but not quite daring to meet the eyes of the assistant as she scuttled from the shop.

The trouble was that these days everyone *glared* at you if you dared smoke a cigarette and Amber was forced to wait until she reached home before she could light up. Whatever happened to personal freedom? she wondered as she slammed the front door behind her and fumbled around for her lighter with shaking hands. She thought about the way Conall Devlin had snatched the cigarette from her lips yesterday and a feeling of fury washed over her.

On a whim, she tapped out a text to her half-brother, Rafe, as she tried to remember what time it was in Australia.

What do you know about a man called Conall Devlin?

Considering they hadn't been in contact for well over a year, Amber was surprised and pleased when Rafe's reply came winging back almost immediately.

Best mate at school. Why?

So *that* was why the name had rung a distant bell and why Conall's midnight-blue eyes had bored into her when he'd said it. Rafe was eleven years older than her and had left home by the time she'd moved back into their father's house as a mixed-up fourteen-year-old. But—come to think of it—hadn't her father mentioned some Irish whizz-kid on the payroll who'd dragged himself up from the gutter? Was Conall Devlin the one he'd been talking about?

She wanted to ask him more, but Rafe was probably lying on some golden beach somewhere, sipping champagne and surrounded by gorgeous women. Did she inform him she was soon to be homeless and that the Irishman had threatened to have the locks changed? Would he even believe her version of the story if he and Conall Devlin had been *best mates*?

There was a ping as another text arrived.

And why are you texting me at midnight?

Amber bit her lip. Was there really any point in grumbling to a man who was thousands of miles away? What was she expecting him to do—transfer money to her account? Because something told her he wouldn't do it, despite the fortune Rafe had built up for himself on the other side of the world. Her half-brother had been one of the people who were always nagging her to get a proper job. Wasn't that one of the reasons why she'd allowed herself to lose touch with him—because he told her things she preferred not hear?

Her fingers wavered over the touchpad.

Just wanted to say hi.

Hi to you, too! Nice to hear from you. Let's talk soon. X

Amber's eyes inexplicably began to fill with tears as she tapped out her reply: Okay. X.

It was the only good thing which had happened to her all day but the momentary glow of contentment it gave her didn't last long. Amber sat on the floor disconsolately finishing her cigarette and then began to shiver. How *could* her father have gone away to India and left her in this predicament?

She thought about what everyone was saying and the different alternatives which lay open to her, realising there weren't actually that many. She could throw herself on people's mercy and ask to sleep on their sofas, but for how long? And she couldn't even do *that* without enough money to offer towards household expenses. Everyone would start to look at her in a funny way if she didn't contribute to food and stuff. And if she couldn't buy her very expensive round in the nightclubs they tended to frequent, then everyone would start to gossip—because in the kind of circles she mixed in, being broke was social death.

She stared down at the diamond watch glittering at her wrist, an eighteenth-birthday present intended to console her during a particularly low point in her life. It hadn't, of course. It had been one of many lessons she'd learnt along the way. It didn't matter how many jewels you wore, their cold beauty was powerless to fill the empty holes which punctured your soul...

She thought about going to a pawnbroker and wondered if such places still existed, but something told her she would get a desultory price for the watch. Because people who tried to raise money against jewellery were vulnerable and she knew better than anyone that the vulnerable were there to be taken advantage of.

The sweat of earlier had dried on her skin and her teeth began to chatter loudly. Amber remembered her father's letter and the words of Mary-Ellen, his assistant. *Speak to Conall Devlin.* And even though every instinct she possessed was warning her to steer clear of the trumped-up Irishman, she suspected she had no choice but to turn to him.

She stared down at her creased clothes.

She licked her lips with a feeling of instinctive fear. She didn't like men. She didn't trust them, and with good reason. But she knew their weaknesses. Her mother hadn't taught her much, but she'd drummed in the fact that men were always susceptible to a woman who looked at them helplessly.

Fired up by a sudden sense of purpose, Amber went into her en-suite bathroom and took a long shower. And then she dressed with more care than she'd used in a long time.

She remembered the disdainful look on Conall Devlin's face when he'd told her that he didn't get turned on by women who smoked and flaunted their bodies. And she remembered the contemptuous expression in his navy-blue eyes as he'd said that. So she fished out a navy-blue dress which she'd only ever worn to failed job interviews, put on minimal make-up and twisted her black hair back into a smooth and demure chignon. Stepping back from the mirror, Amber hardly recognised the image which stared back at her. Why, she could almost pose as a body double for Julie Andrews in *The Sound of Music*!

Conall Devlin's offices were tucked away in a surprisingly picturesque and quiet street in Kensington, which was lined with cherry trees. She didn't know what she'd expected to find, but it certainly hadn't been a restored period building whose outward serenity belied the unmistakable buzz of success she encountered the moment she stepped inside.

The entrance hall had a soaringly high ceiling, with quirky chandeliers and a curving staircase which swept up from the chequered marble floor. A transparent desk sat in front of a modern painting of a woman caressing the neck of a goat. Beside it was a huge canvas with a glittery image of Marilyn Monroe, which Amber recognised instantly. She felt a little stab at her heart. Everything in the place seemed achingly cool and trendy, and suddenly she felt like a fish out of water in her frumpy navy dress and stark hairstyle. A fact which wasn't helped by the lofty blonde receptionist in a monochrome minidress who looked up from behind the Perspex desk and smiled at Amber in a friendly way.

'Hi! Can I help you?'

'I want to see Conall Devlin.' The words came out more clumsily than Amber had intended and the blonde looked a little taken aback.

'I'm afraid Conall is tied up for most of the day,' she said, her smile a little less bright than before. 'You don't have an appointment?'

Amber could feel a rush of emotions flooding through her, but the most prominent of them all was a sensation of being *less than*. As if she had no right to be here. *As if she had no right to be anywhere.* She found herself wondering what on earth she was doing in her frumpy dress when this sunny-looking creature looked as if she'd just strayed in from a land of milk and honey, but it was too late to do anything about it now. She put her bag down on one of the modern chairs which looked more like works of art than objects designed for sitting on, and shot the receptionist a defiant look.

'Not a formal appointment, no. But I need to see him—urgently—so I'll just sit here and wait, if you don't mind.'

The smile now nothing but a memory, a faint frown creased the blonde's brow. 'It might be better if you came back later,' she said carefully.

Amber thought of Conall walking into her apartment without knocking. About the smug look on his face as he'd held up the key and warned her that she had four weeks to get out. She was the sister of his best friend from school, for heaven's sake—surely he could find it in his hard heart to show her a modicum of kindness?

She sat down heavily on one of the chairs.

'I'm not going anywhere. I need to see him and it's urgent, so I'll wait. But please don't worry—I've got all day.' And with that she picked up one of the glossy magazines which were adorning the low table and pretended to read it.

She was aware that the blonde had begun tapping away on her computer, probably sending Conall an email, since she could hardly call him and tell him that a strange woman was currently occupying the reception area and refusing to move—not when she was within earshot.

Sure enough, she heard the sound of a door

opening on the floor above and then someone walking down the sweeping staircase. Amber heard his steps grow closer and closer but she didn't glance up from the magazine until she was aware that someone was coming towards her. And when she could no longer restrain herself, she looked up.

The breath dried in her throat and there wasn't a thing she could do about it, because yesterday she hadn't been expecting him and today she was. And surely that meant she should have been primed not to react—she was busy telling herself *not* to react—but somehow it didn't work like that. Her heart began to pound and her mouth dried to dust and feelings which were completely alien to her began to fizz through her body. On his own territory he looked even more intimidating than he had done yesterday—and that was saying something.

The urbane business suit had gone and he was dressed entirely in black. A black cashmere sweater and a pair of black jeans, which hugged his narrow hips and emphasised his long, muscular legs. His shadowy presence only seemed to emphasise the sense of power which radiated from him like a dark aura.

Against the sombre shade, his skin seemed more golden than she remembered—but his midnight eyes were shuttered and his unsmiling face gave nothing away.

'I thought I told you to make an appointment—although I can't remember if that was before or after you told me to go to hell.' His lips flattened into an odd kind of smile. 'And since you can see for yourself that this place is as far from hell as you can imagine—I'm wondering exactly what it is you're doing here, Amber.'

Amber stared into his eyes and tried to think about something other than the realisation that they gleamed like sapphires. Or that his features were so rugged and strong. He looked so powerful and unyielding, she thought. As if he held all the cards and she held none. She wanted to demand that he listen to her and stop trying to impose his will on her. Until she reminded herself that she was supposed to be appealing to his better nature—in which case it would make sense to adopt a more conciliatory tone, rather than blurting out her demands.

'I've been to the bank,' she said.

He smiled, but it wasn't a particularly

friendly smile. 'And the nasty man there informed you that your father has finally pulled the plug on all the freebies you've survived on until now—is that what you were going to say, Amber?'

'That's exactly what I was going to say,' she whispered.

'And?'

He shot the word out like a bullet and Amber began to wonder if she should have worn something different. Something shorter, which might have shown a bit of leg instead of her knees being completely covered by the frumpy dress.

Well, if you're going to dress like a poor orphan from the storm—then at least start behaving like one.

Her voice gave a little wobble, which wasn't entirely fabricated. 'And I don't know what I'm going to do,' she said.

His lips twisted. 'You could try going out to work, like the rest of the human race.'

'But I...' Amber kept the hovering triumph in her voice at bay and replaced it with a gloomy air of resignation. 'I'm almost impossible to employ, that's the trouble. It's a fierce job market out there and I don't have many of the qualities which employers are seeking.'

'Agreed,' he said unexpectedly. 'An overwhelming sense of entitlement never goes down well with the boss.'

She cleared her throat. 'Things are really bad, Conall. I càn't get hold of my father, my credit cards have all been frozen and I can't... I can't even *eat*,' she finished dramatically.

'But presumably you can still smoke?'

Her head jerked back and her eyes narrowed...

'And don't bother denying it,' he ground out. 'Because I can smell it on you and it makes me sick to the stomach. It's a disgusting habit—and one you're going to have to kick.'

Amber could feel her blood pressure rising, but she forced herself to stay calm. Be docile, she told herself. Let him believe what he wants to believe.

'Of course I'll give it up if you help me,' she said meekly.

'You mean that?'

Chewing on her bottom lip and making her eyes grow very big, Amber nodded. 'Of course I do.'

He gave a brief nod. 'I'm not sure I believe

you, but if you're just playing games, then let me warn you right now that it's a bad idea and you might as well turn around and walk out again. However, if you're really in a receptive place and serious about wanting to change, then I will help you. Do you want my help, Amber?'

It nearly killed her to do so but she gave a sulky nod. 'I suppose so.'

'Good. Then come upstairs to my office and we'll decide what we're going to do with you.' He glanced over at the blonde and Amber was almost certain that he *winked* at her. 'Hold all my calls, will you, Serena?'

CHAPTER THREE

CONALL DEVLIN'S OFFICE was nothing like Amber would have imagined, either. She had expected something brash, or slightly tacky—something which would fit well with his brutish exterior. But she was momentarily lost for words as he took her into a beautifully decorated first-floor room which overlooked the street at the front and a beautiful garden at the back.

The walls were grey—the subtle colour of an oyster shell—and it provided the perfect backdrop for many paintings which hung there. Amber blinked as she looked around. It was like being in an art gallery. He was obviously into modern art and he had a superb eye, she conceded reluctantly. His curved desk looked like a work of art itself and in one corner of the room was a modern sculpture of a naked woman made out of some sort of resin.

Amber glanced over at it before quickly looking away, because there was something uncomfortably *sensual* about the woman's stance and the way she was cupping her breast with lazy fingers.

She looked up to find Conall watching her, his midnight eyes shuttered as he indicated the chair in front of his desk, but Amber was much too wired to be able to sit still while facing him. Something told her that being subjected to that mocking stare would be unendurable.

So start clawing some power back, she told herself fiercely. *Be sweet. Make him* want *to help you.*

He was rich enough to give her a temporary stay of execution until her father got back from his ashram and everything could be cleared up. She walked over to one of the windows and stared down onto the street as two teenage girls strolled past, chewing gum and giggling—and she felt a momentary pang of wistfulness for the apparent ease of their lives and a sense of being carefree which had always eluded her.

'I haven't got all day,' he warned. 'So let's cut to the chase. And before you start fluttering those long eyelashes at me, or trying to work the convent-schoolgirl look—which, let me tell you, isn't doing it for me—let me spell out a few things. I'm not giving you money without something in return and I'm not letting you have an apartment which is way too big for you. So if the sole purpose of this unscheduled visit is to throw yourself on my mercy asking for funds—then you're wasting your time.'

For a moment Amber was struck dumb because she couldn't ever remember anyone speaking to her like that. Up until the age of four she'd been a princess living in a palace, and then she'd been catapulted straight into a nightmare when her parents had split up. The next ten years had been several degrees of horrible and she hadn't known which way to turn. And when she'd been brought back to live in her father's house after her mother's accident—seriously cramping his style with wife number whatever it had been—everyone had tiptoed round her.

Nobody had known how to deal with a grieving and angry teenager and neither had she. Her confidence had been completely punctured and so had her self-esteem. Her moods had been wild and unpredictable and she'd quickly realised that she could get people to do what she wanted them to do. Amber had learnt that if her lips wobbled in a certain way, then people fell over themselves to help her. She'd also realised that rubbing your toe rather obsessively over the carpet and staring at it as if it contained the secret of the universe was pretty effective, too, because it made people want to draw you out of yourself.

But there was something about Conall Devlin which made her realise he would see right through any play-acting or attempts at manipulation. His eyes were much too keen and bright and intelligent. They were fixed on her now in question so that, for one bizarre moment, she felt as if he might actually be able to read her thoughts, and that he certainly wouldn't like them if he could.

'Then how am I expected to survive?' she questioned. Defiantly she held up her wrist so that her diamond watch glittered, like bright sunlight on water. 'Do you want me to start pawning the few valuable items I have?'

His eyes gleamed as he plucked an imaginary violin from the empty air and proceeded to play it, but then he put his big hands down on the surface of his desk and stared at her, his face sombre.

'Why don't you spare me the sob story, Amber?' he said. 'And start explaining some of *these*.'

Suddenly he upended a large manila envelope and spread the contents out over his desk and Amber stared at the collection of photos and magazine clippings with a feeling of trepidation.

'Where did you get these?'

He made an expression of distaste, as if they were harbouring some form of contamination. 'Your father gave them to me.'

Amber knew she'd made it into various gossip columns and some of those 'celebrity' magazines which adorned the shelves of supermarket checkouts. Some of the articles she'd seen and some she hadn't—but she'd never seen them all together like this, like a pictorial history of her life. Fanned across his desk like a giant pack of cards, there were countless pictures of her. Pictures of her leaving nightclubs and pictures of her attending gallery and restaurant openings. In every single shot her dress looked too short and her expression seemed wild. But then the flash of the camera was something that she loved and loathed in equal measure. Wasn't she stupidly grateful that someone cared enough to want to take her photo—as if to reassure her that she wasn't invisible? Yet the downside was that it always made her feel like a butterfly who had fluttered into the collector's room by mistake—who'd had her fragile wings pierced by the sharp pins which then fettered her to a piece of card...

She looked up from the photos and straight into his eyes and nobody could have failed to see the condemnation in their midnight depths. *Don't let him see the chink in your armour*, she told herself fiercely. *Don't give him that power.*

'Quite good, aren't they?' she said carelessly as she pulled out the chair and sat down at last.

At that point, Conall could have slammed his fist onto the desk in sheer frustration, because she was shameless. Completely shameless. Worse even than he'd imagined. Did she think he was stupid—or was the effect of her dressing up today like some off-duty nun supposed to have him eating out of her hand?

But the crazy thing was that—no matter how contrived it was—on some subliminal level, the look actually worked. No matter what he'd said and no matter how much he tried to convince himself otherwise, he couldn't seem to take his eyes off her. With her thick black hair scraped back from her face like that, you could see the perfect oval of her face and get the full impact of those long-lashed emerald eyes. Was she aware that she had the kind of looks which would make men want to fight wars for her? Conall's mouth twisted. Of course she was. And she had been manipulating that beauty, probably since she first hit puberty.

He remembered his reaction when Ambrose had asked him for his help and then shown him all the photos. There had been a moment of stunned silence as Conall had looked at them and felt a powerful hit of lust which had been almost visceral. It had been like a punch to the guts. Or the groin. There had been one in particular of her wearing some wispy little white dress, managing to look both intensely pure and intensely provocative at the same time. Guilt had rushed through him as he'd stared at her father and shaken his head.

'Get someone else to do the job,' he'd said gruffly.

'I can't think of anyone else who would be capable of handling her,' had been Ambrose's candid reply. 'Nor anyone I would trust as much as I do you.'

And wasn't that the worst thing of all? That Ambrose *trusted* him to do right by his daughter? So that, not only had Conall agreed, but he was now bound by a deep sense of honour to do the decent thing by the man who had saved him from a life of crime.

It would have been easier if he could just have signed her a cheque and told her to go away and sort herself out, but Ambrose had been adamant that she needed grounding, and he knew the old man's determination of old.

'She needs to discover how to live a decent life and to stop sponging off other people,' he said. 'And you are going to help her, Conall.'

And how the hell was he supposed to do that when all he could think about was what it would be like to unpin her hair and kiss her until she was gasping for breath? About what it would be like to cradle those hips within the palms of his hands as he drove into her until they were both crying out their pleasure?

He stared into the glitter of her eyes, unable to blot out the unmistakable acknowledgement that her defiance was turning him on even more, because women rarely defied him. So what was he going to do about it—give up or carry on? The question was academic really, because giving up had never been an option for him. Maybe he could turn this into an exercise in self-restraint. Unless his standards had really sunk so low that he could imagine being intimate with someone who stood for everything he most despised.

He thought back to the question she'd just asked and his gaze slid over the pile of photos—alighting on one where she was sitting astride a man's shoulders, a champagne bottle held aloft while a silky green dress clung to her shapely thighs.

'They're good if you want to portray yourself as a vacuous airhead,' he said slowly. 'But then again, that's not something which is going to look good on your CV.'

'Your own CV being whiter than white, I suppose?' she questioned acidly.

For a moment, Conall fixed her with an enquiring look. Had Ambrose told her about the dark blots on his own particular copybook? In which case she would realise that he knew what he was talking about. He'd had his own share of demons; his own wake-up call to deal with. But she said nothing—just continued to regard him with a look of foxy challenge which was making his blood boil.

'This is supposed to be about you,' he said. 'Not me.'

'So go on, then,' she said sarcastically. 'I'm all ears.'

'That's probably the first sensible thing you've said all day.' He leaned back in his chair and studied her. 'This is what I propose you do, Amber. Obviously, you need a job in order to pay the rent but, as you have yourself recognised, your CV makes you unemployable. So you had better come and work for me. Simple.'

Amber went very still because when he put it like that it actually *sounded* simple. She blinked at him as she felt the first faint stirring of hope. Cautiously, she looked around the beautifully proportioned room, with its windows which looked out onto the iconic London street. Outside the trees were frothing with pink blossom, as if someone had daubed them with candyfloss. There was a bunch of flowers on his desk—the tiny, highly scented blooms they called paper-whites, which sent a beguiling drift of perfume through the air. She wondered if the blonde in the minidress had put them there. Just as she wondered who had sent him that postcard of the Taj Mahal, or that little glass dish in the shape of a pair of lips, which was currently home to a gleaming pile of paperclips.

And suddenly she was hit by that feeling which always used to come over her at school, when she was invited to a friend's house for the weekend and the friend's parents were still together. The feeling that she was on the outside looking in at a perfectly ordered world where everything worked the way it was supposed to. She swallowed. Because Conall Devlin was offering her a—temporary—place in that sort of world, wasn't he? Didn't that count for something?

'I'm not exactly sure what your line of business is,' she said, asking the competent kind of question he would no doubt expect.

He regarded her from between those shuttered lashes. 'I deal in property—that's my bread-and-butter stuff. I sell houses and apartments all over London and I have subsidiary offices in Paris and New York. But my enduring love is for art, as you might have gathered.'

'Yes,' she said politely, unable to keep the slight note of amazement from her voice but he picked up on it immediately because his midnight eyes glinted.

'You sound surprised, Amber.'

She shrugged. 'I suppose I am.'

'Because I don't fit the stereotype?' He raised a pair of mocking eyebrows. 'Because my suit isn't pinstriped and I don't have a title?'

'Careful, Mr Devlin—that chip on your shoulder seems like it's getting awfully heavy.'

He laughed at this and Amber was angry with herself for the burst of pleasure which rushed through her. Why the hell feel *thrilled* just because she'd managed to make the over-bearing Irishman laugh?

'I deal solely in twentieth-century pieces and buy mainly for my own pleasure,' he said. 'But occasionally I procure pieces for clients or friends or for business acquaintances. I act as a middle man.'

'Why do they need *you* as a middle man?'

He stared briefly at the postcard of the Taj Mahal. 'Because buying art is not just about negotiation—it's about being able to close the deal. And that's something I'm good at.

Some of the people I buy for are very wealthy, with vast amounts of money at their disposal. Sometimes they prefer to buy anonymously—in order to avoid being ripped off by unscrupulous sellers who want to charge them an astronomical amount.' He smiled. 'Or sometimes people want to sell anonymously and they come to me to help them get the highest possible price.'

Amber's eyes narrowed as she tried not to react to the undeniable impact of that smile. Somehow he had managed to make himself sound incredibly *fascinating*. As if powerful people were keen to do business with him. Had that been his intention, to show her there was more to him than met the eye?

She folded her hands together on her lap. How hard could it be to work for him? The only disadvantage would be having to deal with *him*, but the property side would be a piece of cake. Presumably you just took a prospective buyer along to a house and told them a famous actress had just moved in along the road and prices had rocketed as a result, and they'd be signing on the dotted line quicker than you could say bingo.

'I can do that,' she said confidently.

His eyes narrowed. 'Do what?'

'Sell houses. Or apartments. Whatever you want.'

He sat up very straight. 'Just like that?' he said silkily.

'Sure. How hard can it be?'

'You think I'm going to let someone like you loose in a business I've spent the last fifteen years building up?' he questioned, raking his fingers back through his thick black hair with an unmistakable gesture of irritation. 'You think that selling the most expensive commodity a person will ever buy should be entrusted to someone who hasn't ever held down a proper job, and has spent most of her adult life falling out of nightclubs?'

Amber bristled at his damning assessment and a flare of fury fizzed through her as she listened to his disparaging words. She wanted to do a number of things in retaliation, starting with taking that jug of water from his desk and upending the contents all over his now ruffled dark hair. And then she would have liked to have marched out of his office and slammed the door very firmly behind her and never set eyes on his handsome face ever again. But that wouldn't exactly help foster the brand-new image she was trying to convey, would it? She wanted him to believe she could be calm and unruffled. She would give him a glimpse of the new and efficient Amber who wasn't going to rise to the insults of a man who meant nothing to her, other than as a means to an end.

'I can always learn,' she said. 'But if you think I'd be better suited to shifting a few paintings, I'll happily give that a go. I...I like art.'

He made a small sound at the back of his throat, which sounded almost like a growl, and seemed to be having difficulty holding on to his temper—she could tell that by the way he had suddenly started drumming his fingertips against the desk, as if he were sending out an urgent message in Morse code.

But when he looked up at her again, she thought she saw the glint of something in his dark blue eyes which made her feel slightly nervous. Was it anticipation she could read there, or simply sheer devilment?

'I think you'll find that selling art involves slightly more of a skill set than one described as *shifting a few paintings*,' he said drily. 'And besides, my plans for you are very different.'

He glanced down at the sheet of paper which lay on the desk before him. 'I understand that you speak several languages.'

'Now it's your turn to sound surprised, Mr Devlin.'

He shrugged his broad shoulders and sat back in his seat. 'I guess I am. I didn't have you down as a linguist, with all the hours of study that must have involved.'

Amber's lips flattened. 'There is more than one way to learn a language,' she said. 'My skill comes not from hours sitting at a desk—but from the fact that my mother had a penchant for Mediterranean men. And as a child I often found myself living in whichever new country was the home of her latest love interest.' She gave a bitter laugh. 'And, believe me, there were plenty of those. Consequently, I learnt to speak the local language. It was a question of survival.'

His eyes narrowed as he looked at her thoughtfully. 'That must have been…hard.'

Amber shook her head, more out of habit than anything else. Because sympathy or compassion—or whatever you wanted to call it—made her feel uncomfortable. It started making her remember people like Marco or

Stavros or Pierre—all those men who had broken her mother's heart so conclusively and left Amber to deal with the mess they'd left behind. It made her wish for the impossible—that she'd been like other people and lived a normal, quiet life without a mother who seemed to think that the answer to all their problems was *being in love*. And remembering all that stuff ran the risk of making you feel vulnerable. It left you open to pain—and she'd had more than her fair share of pain.

'It was okay,' she said, in a bored tone which came easily after so many years of practice. 'I certainly know how to say "my darling" in Italian, Greek and French. And I can do plenty of variations on the line "You complete and utter bastard".'

Had her flippant tone shocked him? Was that why a faintly disapproving note had entered his voice?

'Well, you certainly won't be needed to relay any of those sentiments, be very clear about that.' He glanced down at the sheet of paper again. 'But before I lay down the terms of any job I might be prepared to offer—I need some assurances from you.'

'What kind of assurances?'

'Just that I don't have any room in my organisation for loose cannons, or petulant princesses who say the first thing which comes into their head. I deal with people who need careful handling and I need to know that you can demonstrate judgement and tact before I put my proposition to you.' His midnight eyes grew shadowed. 'Because frankly, right now, I'm finding it hard to imagine you being anything other than…difficult.'

His words hurt. More than they should have done. More than she'd expected them to—or perhaps that had something to do with the way he was looking at her. As if he couldn't quite believe the person she was. As if someone like her had no right to exist. And yet all this was complicated by the fact that he looked so spectacular, with his black sweater hugging his magnificent body and his sensual lips making all kinds of complicated thoughts that began to nudge themselves into her mind. Because her body was reacting to him in a way she wasn't used to. A way she couldn't seem to control. She could feel herself growing restless beneath that searing sapphire stare—and yet she didn't even *like* him.

He was like some kind of modern-day *jailer*.

Strutting around in his Kensington mansion with all his skinny, miniskirted minions scurrying around and looking at her as if she were something the cat had dragged in. But she had only herself to blame. He had backed her into a corner and she had let him. She had come crawling here today to ask for his help and he had taken this as permission to give her yet another piece of his mind. Imagine *working* for a man like Conall Devlin.

A familiar sense of rebellion began to well up inside her, accompanied by the liberating realisation that she was under no obligation to accept his dictatorial attitude. Why not show him—and everyone else—that she was a survivor? She might not have a wall covered with degrees, but she wasn't stupid. How hard could it be to find herself a job and a place to live? What about tapping into some of the resilience she'd relied on when she'd been dragged from city to city by her mother?

Rising to her feet, she picked up her handbag, acutely aware of those eyes burning into her as if they were scorching their way through her frumpy navy-blue dress and able to see beneath. And wasn't there something about that scrutiny which excited her as much as terrified her? 'I may be underqualified,' she said, 'but I'm not desperate. I'm resourceful enough to find myself some sort of employment which doesn't involve working for a man with an overinflated sense of his own importance.'

He gave a soft laugh. 'So your answer is no?'

'My answer is more along the lines of *in your dreams*,' she retorted. 'And it's not going to happen. I'm perfectly capable of being independent and that's what I'm going to do.'

'Oh, Amber,' he said slowly. 'You are magnificent. That kind of spirit in a woman is quite something—and if you didn't reek of cigarette smoke and feel that the world owed you some sort of living, you'd be quite worryingly attractive.'

For a moment Amber was confused. Was he insulting her or complimenting her—or was it a mixture of both? She glowered at him before walking over to the door and slamming her way out—to the sound of his soft laughter behind her. But the stupid thing was that she felt like someone who'd jumped out of an aeroplane and forgotten to pull the cord on their parachute. As if she were in free fall. As if the world were rushing up towards her and she didn't know when she was going to hit it.

I'll show them, she told herself fiercely. *I'll show them all.*

CHAPTER FOUR

'I'M SO SORRY!' Quickly, Amber mopped up the spilled champagne and edged away from the table as the customer looked at her with those piggy little eyes which had been trailing her movements all evening. 'I'll get you another drink right away.'

'Why don't you sit down and join me instead?' He leered, patting the seat beside him with a podgy hand. 'And we'll forget about the drink.'

Amber shook her head and tried to hide her ever-present sense of revulsion. 'I'm not supposed to mix with the customers,' she said, grabbing her tray and heading towards the bar on feet which were far from steady. She was used to wearing high heels, but these stilt-like red shoes were so gravity defying that walking in them took every ounce of concentration and it wasn't helped by the rest of the club 'uniform'. Her black satin dress was so tight she could scarcely breathe and meanwhile the heavy throb of the background music was giving her a headache.

And judging by the look on her manager's face, the drink spillage hadn't gone unnoticed. Behind her smile Amber gritted her teeth, wondering if she'd taken leave of her senses when she'd stormed out of Conall's office telling him she didn't want his job. Had she really thought the world would be at her feet, waiting to dole out wonderful opportunities by way of compensation? Because life wasn't like that. She'd quickly discovered that a CV riddled with holes and zero qualifications brought you few opportunities and the only work available was in places like this—an underlit hotel nightclub where nobody looked happy.

'That's the third drink you've spilled this week!' The manager's voice quivered indignantly as Amber grew closer. 'Where did you learn to be so clumsy?'

'I...I moved a bit too quickly. I thought he was going to pinch my bottom,' babbled Amber.

'And? What's the matter with that?' The manager glared. 'Isn't it nice to have a man show his appreciation towards an attractive woman? Why else do you think we dress you up like that? Well, you'll have the cost of the drink taken from your wages, Amber. Now go and fetch him another one and, for goodness' sake, try and be a bit friendlier this time.'

Amber could feel her heart thudding as the bartender put a fresh glass of fizzy wine masquerading as champagne on her tray and she began to walk back towards the man with piggy eyes. *Just put the drink down carefully and then leave*, she told herself. But as she bent down in front of him, he reached out to curve his fat fingers around her fishnet-covered thigh and she froze.

'What…what are you doing?' she croaked.

'Oh, come on.' He leered at her again. 'No need to be like that. With legs like that it's a crime not to touch them—and you look like you could do with a square meal. So how about we go up to my room after you finish? You can order something from room service and we can—'

'How about you get your filthy hand off her right now, before I knock you into kingdom come?' came a low and furious voice from behind her, which Amber recognised instantly.

The podgy hand fell away and Amber turned around to see Conall standing there—his rugged face a study in fury and his powerful body radiating adrenaline as he dominated the space around him. The lurch of trepidation she felt at his unexpected appearance was quickly overridden by the disturbing realisation that she'd never been so glad to see someone in her whole life. He looked so strong. So powerful. He made every other man in the room look weak and insubstantial. Her heart began to pound and she felt her mouth grow dry.

'Conall!' she whispered. 'What are you doing here?'

'Well, I certainly haven't come here for a quiet drink. I tend to be a little more discerning in my choice of venue.' Raising his voice against the loud throb of music, he glanced around at the other cocktail waitresses with a shudder of distaste he didn't bother to hide. 'Get your coat, Amber. We're leaving.'

'I can't leave. I'm working.'

'Not here, you aren't. Not any more. And the subject isn't up for discussion, so save your breath. Either you come willingly, or I pick you up and carry you out of here in a fireman's lift. The choice,' he finished grimly, 'is yours.'

Amber wondered if there was something wrong with her—there must be—because why else would the thought of the Irishman putting her over his shoulder make her heart race even harder than it was already? She could see her manager saying something to a burly-looking man who was standing beside the bar, and as the music continued its relentless beat she began to dread some awful scene. What if Conall got into a fight with Security—with fists and glasses flying?

'I'll get my coat,' she said.

'Do it,' he bit out impatiently. 'And hurry up. This place is making my skin crawl.'

She headed for the changing room—relieved to strip off the minuscule satin dress and fishnet tights and kick the scarlet shoes from her aching feet. Her skin was clammy and briefly she splashed her face with cold water, dabbing herself dry with a paper towel before slithering into jeans and a sweater. Her heart was racing when she reappeared in the club—thankful to find Conall still standing there, with the bar manager handing over what looked like a wad of cash, with a sour expression on her face.

'Let's go,' he said as she approached.

'Conall—'

'Not now, Amber,' he snapped. 'I really don't want to have a conversation with you here, in earshot of all this low life.'

His expression was resolute and his determination undeniable—so what choice did she have but to follow him through the weaving basement corridors of the hotel until they found the elevator which took them to the main lobby?

They emerged into the dark crispness of a clear spring night and Amber sucked in a lungful of clean air as a chauffeur-driven car purred to a halt beside the kerb.

'Get in,' said Conall and she wondered if he'd spent his whole life barking out orders like that.

But she did as he asked and a feeling of being cocooned washed over her the moment she climbed onto the back seat, because this level of luxury was reassuringly familiar. A luxury she'd been able to count on before Conall and her father had conspired to take it away from her. She glanced over at his hard profile as he got into the car beside her, and her temporary gratitude began to dissolve into a feeling of resentment.

'How did you find me?' she demanded as the powerful engine began to purr into life.

He turned to look at her and, despite the dim light of the car's interior, the angry glitter in his eyes was unmistakable. 'I had one of my people keep track of you.'

'Why?'

'Why do you think? Because you're so damned irresistible I couldn't keep away from you? I hoped I might be able to tell your father how well you were doing following your dramatic exit from my office.' He gave a short laugh. 'Some hope. I should have guessed that you'd head for the tackiest venue in town in search of some easy money.'

'So why bother coming to look for me if you'd already written me off as useless?' she flared.

Conall didn't answer straight away, because his own motives were still giving him cause for concern. He'd been worried about her ability to adapt to a hard world without the cushion of her wealth—yes. And he'd heard stuff about the club where she was working which made him feel uneasy. Yes. That, too. But there had been something more—something which wasn't quite so easy to quantify—which had nothing to do with his moral debt to her father. Hadn't there been a part of him which had admired the way she'd flounced out of his office? And he didn't just mean the pleasure of watching the magnificent sway of her curvy bottom as she'd done so. The way she'd turned down his offer of a job with a flash of defiance in those emerald eyes had made him think that maybe there was a strong streak of pride hidden beneath her wilful surface. He'd imagined her scrubbing floors, doing anything rather than having to work for him, and he couldn't deny that the idea had appealed to him.

He had been wrong, of course. She had gone for the easy solution. The quick fix. She'd seized the first opportunity to shoehorn her magnificent body into a dress which left very little to the imagination and work in a place which attracted nothing but low life. Clearing his throat, he tried to wipe from his mind the memory of those magnificent breasts spilling over the top of the tight satin gown, but the hard aching in his groin was proving more stubborn to control.

'I felt a certain responsibility towards you.'

'Because of my father?'

'Of course. Why else?'

'Another of Daddy's yes-men,' she said tonelessly.

'Oh, I'm nobody's yes-man, Amber. Be very clear about that.' His voice sounded steely. 'And ask yourself what would have happened if I hadn't turned up when I had. Or have I got it all wrong? Maybe you liked that creep pawing your thigh like that? Maybe you couldn't wait to get back to his room for him to give you a "square meal".'

'Of course I didn't! He was a complete creep. They all were.'

He shook his head in exasperation. 'So why the hell couldn't you have taken a normal job? Worked in a shop? Or a café?'

'Because shops and cafés don't provide accommodation! And the club said if I worked a successful month's trial, then I could have one of the staff rooms in the hotel! Which would have coincided neatly with me being evicted from my apartment.' She glared at him. 'And I don't know why you're suddenly trying to sound like the voice of concern when it's *your* fault I'm going to be homeless.'

He gave an impatient sigh. 'I can't believe you'd be so naïve. You must realise how these places operate.'

'I've been to more nightclubs than you've had hot dinners!' she retorted.

'I don't doubt it—but you went there as a rich and valued customer, not a member of staff! Places like that exploit beautiful women. They expect you to *earn* your bonuses—in a way which is usually some variation of lying flat on your back. Haven't you ever heard the expression that there's no such thing as a free lunch?'

The way she was biting on her lip told him that maybe she wasn't as sophisticated as her foxy appearance suggested, or maybe her wealth had always ensured that she'd frequented a classier kind of club, up until now. Unwillingly, he let his gaze drift over her and once he had started, he couldn't seem to stop. Her black hair was spilling down over the shoulders of her raincoat and her green eyes were heavy with make-up. The fading scarlet streak of her lipstick matched those killer heels she'd been wearing when he'd watched her sashaying across the bar, making him have the sort of unwanted erotic thoughts which involved having her ankles wrapped very tightly around his neck. Hell, it would be easy to have those kinds of thoughts even now—even when she was bundled up in an all-concealing raincoat.

He tapped his fingers against one taut thigh. It would be better to wash his hands of her. To tell Ambrose that she was pretty much a lost cause and maybe he would just have to accept that and let her carry on with an open cheque-book and a life of pure indulgence.

But as the car passed a lamp post and the light splashed over her face, he noticed for the first time the dark shadows beneath her long-lashed eyes. She looked as if she hadn't had a lot of sleep lately—and she'd lost weight. Her cheekbones were shockingly prominent in her porcelain skin and the belted raincoat drew definition to the narrowness of her waist. She looked as if a puff of wind might blow her away. As if on cue, her stomach began to rumble and he frowned.

'When did you last eat?'

Her expression was mulish. 'What do you care?'

'Stop being so damned stubborn and just answer the question, Amber,' he growled.

She shrugged. 'At the club they advised you not to eat for at least four hours before your shift. Actually, it was pretty sound advice because it seemed to be club policy to give you a uniform dress which was at least one size too small.'

'And do you have food back in your apartment?'

'Not much,' she admitted.

'Spent it all on cigarettes, I suppose?' he accused.

She didn't correct him as he leaned forward to tap the glass panel which divided them from the chauffeur and the panel slid open.

'Take us to my club,' he commanded.

'Conall, I'm tired,' she objected. 'And I want to go home.'

'Tough. You can sleep afterwards. You need to eat something.'

He didn't say anything more until the car drew up outside the floodlit classical building a short distance from Piccadilly Circus. A uniformed porter sprang forward to open the car door to let her get out and Conall felt a stab of something he couldn't decipher as he followed her sexy sway as she made her way up the marble steps. As she handed over her raincoat he thought he saw her shiver and he took his own cashmere scarf and wound it around her neck, leaving the ends to dangle conceal-ingly in front of her magnificent breasts.

'Better wear this,' he said drily. But it was more for his benefit than any attempt to con-form to the club's rather outdated dress code. This way he wouldn't have to look at the pin-point tips of her nipples thrusting their way towards him from beneath her sweater and making him imagine what it would be like to lock his lips around each one in turn.

It was very late, but they were shown into the long room known as the North Library which overlooked Pall Mall, where a table was quickly laid up for them. Conall ordered soup and sandwiches for Amber and a brandy for himself. He watched in silence as she de-voured the comfort food with the undivided attention of someone who was genuinely hun-gry and, for the first time that evening, he began to relax.

He sipped his drink. Outside the busy city was slowing down. He could see the yellow lights of vacant cabs and the unsteady weave of people making their way home, while in here all was ordered and calm. It always was. It was one of the main reasons why he'd joined, because it had an air of stability which had always attracted him.

Antique chandeliers hung from the corniced ceiling and at one end of the room was a polished grand piano. Despite its traditional air, it was a club for movers and shakers—the kind of place to which few were granted entry because the membership requirements were so high. But there had been no shortage of proposers keen to get him onto the members' list and Conall had defied the odds brought about by youthful misdemeanour. He'd been proposed by a government minister and seconded by a peer of the realm and that fact in itself still had the ability to make him smile wryly. Whoever would have thought that the boy who had been born with so little would end up here, with the great and the good?

He signalled for a fire to be lit and then watched as Amber dabbed at her lips with a heavy linen napkin. Now that the edge had been taken off her hunger, she relaxed back into the leather armchair and began to look around—like a rescued kitten which had been brought from the cold into the warmth. He wondered what the waiter who came to remove her plate must think, because he didn't usually bring women here, to this essentially male enclave—where deals were done over dinner and alliances formed over summer drinks taken outside on the pretty terrace. On the rare occasions he'd brought a date, they hadn't been dressed in skinny jeans and a sweater, like Amber Carter. They had worn subtle silk, with shoes the same colour as their handbags and make-up which was soft and discreet—not laden on so thickly that from a distance she appeared to have two black eyes.

And yet not one of them had made him feel a fraction of the desire which was currently pulsing through his blood and making him achingly aware of his erection.

'So,' he said heavily, putting his glass down on the table and raising his eyebrows in what he hoped was a stern expression. 'I think you've just proved fairly conclusively that independence is not an option—unless you want to take another job like that. The question is whether or not you're finally ready to knuckle down and see sense.'

Amber didn't answer straight away, even though he was firing that impatient look at her. She felt much better after the food she'd just eaten, no doubt about it—but just as one hunger had been satisfied, so another had been awoken and she wasn't sure how to deal with it.

It wasn't just the unexpectedness of seeing Conall Devlin in this famous London club—which, quite frankly, was the last place she'd ever imagined finding someone like him. And it wasn't just the fact that he currently resembled the human equivalent of a jungle cat—a dark and potentially dangerous predator who had temporarily taken refuge in one of the beautifully worn leather chairs. No, it was more than that. It was the subtly pervasive scent of him invading her nostrils, which was coming from the soft scarf he'd draped around her neck. And hadn't she felt a whisper of pleasure when his fingertips had brushed against her skin, even though it had been the most innocent of touches? Hadn't it made her want more, even though experience had taught her that she always froze into a block of ice whenever a man came close?

She looked into the gleam of his eyes. 'By seeing sense, I presume you mean I should do exactly what *you* say?'

'Well, you could give it a try,' he said drily.

'Since we've seen what happens when you do the opposite.'

'But I don't know exactly what it is you're offering me, Conall.'

Conall stiffened. Was he imagining the provocative flash of her eyes—or was that just wishful thinking on his part? Was she aware that when she looked at him that way, his veins were pulsing with a hot, hard hunger and he could think of only one way of relieving it? She must be. Women like her ate men like him for breakfast.

He needed to pull himself together, before she got an inkling of the erotic thoughts which were clogging up his mind and started using her sexual power to manipulate him. 'I'm offering you a role as an interpreter.'

'Not interested,' she said instantly, with an emphatic shake of her head. 'I'm not sitting in some claustrophobic booth all day with a pair of headphones on, while someone jabbers on and on in my ear about something boring— like grain quotas in the European Union.'

Conall failed to hide his smile. 'I think you'll find my proposal is a little more glamorous than that,' he said.

'Oh?'

She had perked up now and his smile died. Of course she had. Glamour was her lifeblood, wasn't it?

'I'm having a party,' he said.

'What kind of party?'

He picked up his brandy glass and took a sip. 'A party ostensibly to celebrate the completion of my country house. There will be music, and dancing—but I'm also hoping to use the opportunity to sell a painting for someone who badly needs the money.'

'I thought you'd decided that, with my lack of experience, I would be useless when it came to selling paintings.'

'I'm not expecting you to *sell* the paintings,' he said. 'I just want you to be there as a sort of linguistic arm candy.'

'What do you mean?'

He hesitated, wondering if her father would approve of the offer he was about to make to her. It would probably be more sensible to give her a lowly back-room job somewhere in his organisation—preferably as far away from him as possible. But Conall could see now that it would be as ineffective as trying to pass fish paste off as caviar, because Amber Carter wasn't a back-room kind of woman.

No way could someone like her ever fade into the background. So why not capitalise on the gifts she *did* have?

'The painting in question is one of a pair,' he said. 'Two studies of the same woman by a man called Kristjan Wheeler—a contemporary of Picasso and an artist whose worth has increased enormously over the last decade. Both pictures went missing in the middle of the last century and only one has ever been found. That is the one I am trying to sell on behalf of my client, and...'

She looked at him as his words tailed away. 'And?'

'I believe the man who wants to buy the painting is in possession of the missing picture. Which means that the one I'm selling is part of a set, and naturally that makes it much more valuable.'

'Can't you just ask him outright whether he's got it?'

He gave the flicker of a smile. 'That's not how negotiation works, Amber—and especially not with a man like this.' He watched her closely. 'You see, the prospective buyer is a prince.'

'A *prince*?'

Conall watched as she sat bolt upright, her fingers tightening around her glass. Her lips had parted and he could see the moist gleam of her tongue. He thought she looked like a starving dog which had been allowed to roam freely around a kitchen and a quiver of distaste ran through him. He took another sip of his brandy. Had he really thought that the chemistry which sizzled between them was unique? Or was he naïvely pretending that she wasn't like this with every man she came across, and the higher that man's status and the fatter his wallet, the better?

And yet surely that would make her perfect for what he had in mind—didn't they say that Luciano of Mardovia had a roving eye where women were concerned?

'That's right,' he said, his eyes narrowing. 'I want you to come to the party and be nice to him.'

Her eyes narrowed. 'How nice?'

The inference behind her question was clear and Conall felt a wave of disgust wash over him. 'I'm not expecting you to have sex with him,' he snapped. 'Just chat to him. Dance with him. Charm him. I shouldn't imagine you would find any of that difficult, given your track record. He will be accompanied by at least two of his aides and he will converse with them in any language except English. Just like you he speaks Italian, Greek and French and he certainly won't be expecting a woman like you to be fluent in all three.'

A woman like you.

It was odd how hurtful Amber found his throwaway comment, especially when for a minute back then she had been lulled into a false sense of security. Secretly, she had *enjoyed* the way he'd turned up and taken her away so masterfully. He'd brought her here— to this club, which was the epitome of elegance and comfort—and she couldn't deny that she was enjoying watching him sitting bathed in flickering firelight, while he sipped at his brandy. He was very easy on the eye.

But she needed to remember that for him she was just a burden. A problem to be dealt with and then disposed of. No point in starting to have fantasies about Conall Devlin.

'So what you're saying, in effect, is that you want me to spy on this Prince?'

He didn't seem particularly bothered by her accusation, for he responded with nothing more than a faintly impatient sigh.

'Don't be so melodramatic, Amber. If I asked you to have a business meeting with a competitor, I would expect you to find out as much information as possible. So if the Prince should happen to comment to one of his aides in, say, Greek that the wine is atrocious, then it would be helpful to know that.'

A smile flickered over her lips. 'You're in the habit of serving atrocious wine, are you, Conall?'

'What do you think?'

'I'm thinking...no.'

'Look, I'm not asking you to lie about your language skills, but there's no need to advertise them. This is business. All I want is to get the best price possible for my client—and Luciano can certainly afford to pay the best price. So...' His midnight gaze swept over her. 'Do you think you can do it? Play hostess for me for an evening and stick to the Prince's side like glue?'

Amber met his eyes. The food and the fire and the brandy had made her feel sleepy and safe and part of her wished she could hold on to this moment and not have to go and face the chill of the outside world. But Conall was clearly waiting for an answer to his question and the expression on his face suggested he wasn't a man who enjoyed being kept waiting. And deep down she knew she could do something like this in her sleep. Go to some upmarket party and be charming? Child's play.

'Yes,' she said. 'I can do it.'

'Good.' He nodded as his cell phone gave a discreet little buzz and he flicked it a brief glance. 'You'll need to get down to my country house early on Saturday afternoon. Oh, and bring some party dresses with you.' His eyes glittered. 'I don't imagine you'll have too much trouble finding any of those in your wardrobe?'

'No. Party dresses I have in abundance— and plenty of shoes to match.'

'Just wear something halfway decent, will you?'

'What *do* you mean?'

'You know damned well what I mean.' There was a pause. 'I don't want you flaunting your body and looking like a tramp.'

Amber swallowed, knowing that she should be outraged by such a statement, and yet something about the way he said it made her feel all…shivery. She forced her mind back to the practical. 'So what time will I expect the car?'

'The car?' he repeated blankly.

'The car which will be collecting me,' she said, as if she were explaining the rules of a simple card game to a five-year-old.

There was a short silence before he tipped back his dark head and laughed, but when he looked at her again his eyes weren't amused, they were stone cold. 'You still don't get it, do you, Amber?' he said. 'You may be about to deal with a prince, but you're going to have to stop behaving like a princess. Because you're not. You will catch the train like any other mortal. Speak to Serena and she'll give you details of how to find the house. Oh, and I've got your wages from the nightclub in my pocket. I'll give them to you in the car. I didn't want to hand them over in here.' His eyes glittered. 'It could be a gesture open to misinterpretation.'

CHAPTER FIVE

AMBER HADN'T BEEN on a train for years. Not since that time in Rome when her mother's lover had confessed to having a pregnant wife who had just discovered their affair and was on the warpath. It had been bad enough having to flee the city leaving behind half their possessions, but the journey had been made worse by Sophie Carter's increasingly hysterical sobs as she'd exclaimed loudly that she would be unable to live without Marco. It had been left to her daughter to try to placate her, to the accompaniment of tutting sounds from the other people in the carriage.

Amber sat back against the hard train seat and thought about the bizarre twists and turns of life which had brought her to this bumpy carriage which was hurtling through the English countryside towards Conall's country home. She had been corralled into working for the Irish tycoon—the most infuriating and high-handed man she'd ever met.

And the fact that there didn't seem any credible alternative had made her examine her lifestyle in a way which had left her feeling distinctly uncomfortable.

Yesterday she'd gone to the Devlin headquarters in Kensington for a briefing which hadn't been brief at all. Serena had spent ages telling her boring things like making sure she kept her receipts so that she could submit a travel expenses form. Amber remembered blinking at Conall's assistant with a mixture of amusement and irritation. Receipts! She had wanted to tell the lofty blonde that she didn't *do* receipts, but at that moment the great man himself had walked into the building—a distracting image dressed in all black. Cue an infuriating rocketing of Amber's pulse and the spectacle of various female members of staff cooing around him. And cue the uncomfortable realisation that she *didn't like* seeing him surrounded by all those women.

His gaze had met hers.

'I hope you're behaving yourself, Amber?'

'I'm doing my best,' she'd replied from between gritted teeth.

'I'm just talking Amber through the expenses procedure,' Serena had explained.

'And I'm sure she has been nothing but completely cooperative,' Conall had murmured in response, but there had been a definite flicker of warning in the sapphire depths of his eyes.

She'd wanted to defy him then, because defiance was her default mechanism, yet for the first time in her life she had come up against someone who would not be swayed by her. And wasn't that in some crazy way—*reassuring*?

Amber stared out of the train window, realising there was only an hour to go before her journey's end and that she had better be prepared for her meeting with the Prince. Conall had suggested she find out as much about the royal as possible and so she had downloaded as much as she could find on the Internet and had printed it out. No harm in looking at it again. She pulled out the information sheets and began to doodle little drawings around the edge of one of the pages as she reread it.

She had been unprepared for the impact of Prince 'Luc' and his gorgeous Mediterranean island, when his photograph had first popped up on the screen. With his olive skin, bright blue eyes and thick tumble of black hair, he was as handsome as any Hollywood actor, but his looks left her completely cold. That in itself wasn't unusual, because she'd met enough manipulating hunks through her mother to put her off handsome men for ever. What *was* infuriating was that she kept unfavourably comparing the Prince to Conall—and yet Conall wasn't what you'd call *good-looking*. His jaw was dark and his nose had been broken at one point. And he had a hard, cold stare, which proved distractingly at odds with the way his fingers had brushed her skin as he'd wound his scarf around her neck at his club the other night…

The train juddered to a halt at Crewhurst station and Amber climbed out onto the platform, clutching her case, which contained some of her less-revealing dresses. Blinking, she looked around her and breathed in the fresh air, the bright spring day making her feel like an animal who'd spent the winter in hibernation and was emerging into sunshine for the first time. She sniffed at the air and the scent of something sweet. She couldn't remember the last time she'd been out of the city and in the middle of the countryside like this. Cotton-wool clouds scudded across an eggshell-blue sky and frilly yellow daffodils waved their trumpets in the light breeze.

She had been told to take a taxi, but the rank was empty and when she asked the old man in the ticket office when one might be available, he shook his head with the expression of someone who had just been asked to provide the whereabouts of the Holy Grail.

'Can't say. Driver's gone off to take his wife shopping. It isn't far to walk,' he added helpfully, when she told him where she was headed.

Under normal circumstances Amber would have tapped her foot impatiently and demanded that someone find her a taxi—and quickly. But there was something about the scent of spring which felt keen and raw on her senses. She couldn't remember the last time she'd felt this *alive* and a sudden feeling of adventure washed over her. Her bag wasn't particularly heavy. She was wearing sneakers with her skinny jeans, wasn't she? And a soft silk shirt beneath her denim jacket.

After taking directions, she set off along a sun-dappled country road, walking past acid-green hedges which were bursting with new life. Overhead the sound of birdsong was almost deafening and London seemed an awfully long way away. She found herself thinking that Conall seemed to have his life pretty much sorted, with his successful business and his homes in London and the country. And she found herself wondering whether or not he had a girlfriend. Probably. Men like him always had girlfriends. Or wives. A wife who presumably could only speak English.

This thought produced an inexplicably painful punch to her heart and she glanced at her watch, calculating she must be about halfway there when she noticed that the sky had grown dark. Looking up, she saw a bank of pewter clouds massing overhead and increased her speed, but she hadn't got much further down the lane when the first large splash of rain hit her and she wondered why she hadn't stopped to consider the April showers which came out of nowhere this time of year.

Because usually you're never far from a shop doorway and completely protected from the elements, that's why.

Well, she certainly wasn't protected now.

She was alone in the middle of a country lane while the rain had started lashing down with increasing intensity, until it was almost like walking through a tropical storm. She thought about ringing someone. Conall? No. She didn't want another lecture on her general incompetence. And it was hardly the end of the world to get caught in an April shower, was it? Sometimes you had to accept what fate threw at you, and just suck it up.

Thoroughly soaked now, she increased her pace, her shirt clinging to her breasts like wet tissue paper and her jeans feeling heavy and uncomfortable as the wet denim rubbed against her legs. She didn't hear the car at first and it wasn't until she heard a loud beep that she turned around to see a low black car coming to a halt on the wet lane with a soft screech of tyres. The muscular silhouette behind the wheel was disturbingly familiar and as the electric window floated down she was confronted by the sight of Conall's face and her heart missed a beat.

'Conall—'

'Get in,' he said.

For a moment she was tempted to tell him that she'd rather walk in the pouring rain than get in a car driven by *him*. But that would be stupid—and wasn't she trying her best to be a bit more sensible? She was cold and she was wet and she was headed for his house and the grown-up thing to do would be to thank him for stopping. Pulling open the passenger door, she threw her bag on the floor, beginning to shiver violently as she slid onto the passenger seat and slammed the car door shut.

'This is getting to be something of a habit,' he said grimly. 'Do you think I have the words "rescue mission" permanently stamped on my forehead?'

His rudeness made her polite response disintegrate. 'I didn't ask you to rescue me.'

'But you accepted my help soon enough, didn't you?'

'Because even I'm not stubborn enough to throw up the chance of getting into a warm car! And now I s-suppose you're going to ch-chastise me for getting wet.' She began to shiver. 'As if I have any control over the weather!'

'I was going to chastise you for walking in the middle of the damned road and not paying any attention!' he retorted. 'If I'd been going any faster I could have run you over.'

Her teeth had started to chatter loudly and the way he was looking at her was making her feel... Beneath her sopping silk shirt, Amber's heart began to hammer. She didn't want to think about the way he was making her feel. How could that cold blue stare make her body spring into life like this? How could it make her feel as if her breasts were being pierced by tiny little needles and make a slow melting heat unfurl deep in her belly?

But he was tugging off his leather jacket and draping it impatiently over her shoulders and as his shadow fell over her Amber was suddenly aware of just how close he was. Coal-black lashes framed the gleaming sapphire eyes and his deeply shadowed jaw seemed to emphasise his own very potent brand of masculinity. An unfamiliar sense of longing began to bubble up inside her and she held her breath as she looked up into his face. For a split second she thought he might be about to kiss her. A second when his mouth was so close that all she needed to do was reach up and hook her hand behind his neck, and bring those lips down to meet hers. And in that same second she saw his eyes narrow. She thought... thought...

Did he read the longing in her eyes? Was that why he suddenly pulled away with a hard smile, as if he'd known exactly what was going through her head? Maybe he was able to make women desire him, even if they didn't want to, just by giving them that intense and rather smouldering look. Instinctively, she hugged the coat closer, the leather feeling unbearably soft against her erect and sensitised nipples.

'Do up your seat belt,' he ordered, turning up the car's heater full blast and glancing in his rear mirror before pulling away. 'And talk me through the reason why you decided to walk from the station. It's miles.'

'Why do you think? Because there was no taxi and the man at the ticket office said it wasn't far.'

'You should have rung me.'

'Make your mind up, Conall. You can't criticise me for not behaving like a normal person and then moan at me when I do. I thought it would be good for me to make my way to the house independently. I thought you might even award me a special gold star for good behaviour.' She glanced at him, a smile playing around her lips. 'And to be honest, I didn't know you were already there.'

Conall said nothing as the car made its way through the downpour, the rhythmical swishing of the wiper blades the only sound he could hear above his suddenly erratic breathing. Of course she hadn't known he'd be at the house—he hadn't known himself. He'd planned to arrive later when everything was in place but something had compelled him to get here earlier, and that something was making him uncomfortable because it was all to do with her.

He'd tried telling himself that he needed to oversee the massive security detail which the Prince of Mardovia's bodyguards had demanded prior to the royal visit. That he needed to check on the painting he was hoping to sell and to ensure it was properly lit. But although both those reasons were valid, they weren't the real reason why he was desperately trying to avert his gaze from the damp denim which outlined the slenderness of her thighs.

Admit it, he thought grimly. *You want her. Despite everything you know about her, you haven't been able to get her out of your head since you saw her lying on a white leather sofa wearing that baggy T-shirt.* Only now the image searing into his brain was the way her wet silk shirt had been clinging to her peaking breasts before he'd hastily covered them up with his jacket. Was it shocking to admit that he wanted to rip the delicate fabric aside and lick her on each hard nub until she squirmed with pleasure? To slide the damp denim from her thighs and put his heated hands all over her chilled flesh?

Of course it was shocking. He had been entrusted to look after her, not seduce her. If it was sex he wanted then Eleanor was only a phone call away. Their grown-up and civilised 'friends with benefits' relationship suited them both—even if the physical stimulation it gave him wasn't matched by a mental one.

But for once the thought of Eleanor's blonde beauty paled in the face of the fiery, green-eyed temptress on the seat next to him and he was relieved when the sudden shower began to lessen. The sun broke through the clouds as the car made its way up the long drive, just in time to illuminate his house in a radiant display which emphasised its stately proportions. Golden light washed over the tall chimneys and glinted off the mullioned windows. The emerald lawns surrounding the building looked vivid in the bright sunshine and, on a tranquil pond, several ducks quacked happily. Beside him he felt Amber stiffen.

'But this is…this is *beautiful*,' she breathed as the car drew up outside.

He heard the note of wonder in her voice and his mouth hardened. He wondered if she would have been quite so gushing if she'd known the truth about his background. About the hardship and pain and the sense of being an outsider which had never quite left him.

'Isn't it?' he agreed evenly as he stared at the house. With its acres of parkland and sense of history, places like this didn't come on the market very often and Conall still couldn't quite believe it was his. Coming hot on the heels of his London deal, it had been a heady time in terms of recent property acquisitions. Had he ever imagined being a major land-owner, when he was eighteen and mad with rage and injustice? When the walls of the detention centre had threatened to close in on him and he had been looking down the barrel of an extended jail sentence?

He turned off the ignition, his glance straying to Amber's large handbag, and it wasn't the sight of the printout about Prince Luciano which caught his eye—although he was pleased to see she'd been doing her home-work—but the intricate doodles on the edge of one of the pages which stirred a faint but enduring memory.

He frowned. 'I remember seeing some drawings like this in your apartment that first day.'

She stiffened. 'What, you mean you were snooping around?'

'They were half hidden behind a sofa. Were they yours?'

'Of course they were mine—why?'

Ignoring the defensive note in her voice, he narrowed his eyes. 'I thought some of them showed real promise and a few were really very good.'

'You don't have to say that. Anyway, I know they're rubbish.'

'I don't say things I don't mean, Amber. And why are they rubbish?'

She shrugged, but the words seemed to take a long time coming. 'I used to paint a lot when we were in Europe and my mother was otherwise *occupied*. But when I went to live with my father, he made it very clear he thought they were no good—that a kid of six could throw some paint at the canvas and get the same effect, and that I was wasting my time.' She flashed a brittle kind of smile. 'So I stopped trying to be an *artist* and became the society girl that everyone expected. Those paintings you saw were years old. I just…just couldn't bear to throw them away.'

Conall experienced a moment of real, silent rage as he read the brief flash of hurt and helplessness in her eyes. Were adults deliberately cruel to troubled teenagers, or was it simply that they didn't know how to handle them?

But maybe she'd always been difficult to handle—in so many ways. Right now she looked like every teenage boy's fantasy in her wet shirt, with his bulky jacket draped around her slender shoulders, making far too many lustful thoughts crowd his mind. 'I'll show you around the house so you have plenty of time to acclimatise yourself before the party, but the guided tour can wait until later. First you need to get out of those wet clothes.'

As soon as the words had left his lips he wanted to take them back, because they sounded like the words a man would say to a woman just before he began touching her. Silently chastising himself for his own foolishness, he got out of the car and opened the door for her.

Still hugging his jacket to her, Amber followed him inside the house into a huge oak-panelled hallway from which curved a majestic staircase. Enormous bucketfuls of white flowers stood on the floor, obviously waiting to be transplanted into vases, and she could hear the sound of female voices coming from a room somewhere and a radio playing in the distance.

'Last-minute party prep,' he said, in reply to a question she hadn't asked. 'You'll meet the team later. Now come with me and I'll show you to your room.'

Her clothes were still clinging damply to her body and Amber guessed she should have been cold—but cold was the last thing she felt right now. Her blood felt heavy and warm as she followed Conall upstairs and her heart was beating painfully against her ribcage. She barely noticed the beautifully restored woodwork or the walls covered with paintings, so fixated was she on the hard thrust of his buttocks against the black denim of his jeans. She could feel her throat growing dry as she stared at the back of his neck, unable to tear her gaze away. With his black hair curling over the collar of his cashmere sweater and his muscular physique rippling with health and strength, he looked in total command of the situation, which she guessed he was. But the weird thing was that she didn't *do* this. She didn't drool over men who treated her as if she were a naughty schoolgirl. Truth was, she didn't drool over anyone. She bit her lip as she remembered the accusations which had been levelled at her in the past. *Cold. Frigid. Ice queen.* Valid accusations, every one of them. Yet when Conall looked at her, he made her want to melt, not freeze.

Pushing open the door of a second-floor bedroom overlooking the parkland at the back of the house, he put her case down. 'You should be comfortable enough in here,' he said abruptly.

Amber glanced around, suddenly shy to find herself alone in a bedroom with him. Comfortable was an understatement for such a lavish room and she was grateful he'd given her somewhere so lovely to sleep, with its heavy velvet drapes and enormous four-poster bed. She looked up into his face, knowing she ought to be asking intelligent questions about the forthcoming party but it was difficult when all she could think about was the curve of his lips and the shadowed roughness of his jaw.

'What time do you need me?' she said, her

words sounding jerky as she moistened the roof of her mouth with her tongue.

'Come downstairs at around seven and I'll show you the painting. The Prince is arriving at eight-fifteen and his timetable is worked out to the nearest second. I'd better warn you that lateness won't be tolerated when you're dealing with royals.'

'I won't be late, Conall.' Amber took off his jacket and handed it to him, feeling chilled as the leather left her skin and missing the subtle scent which was all his. 'And thanks for lending me this.'

But he didn't take the jacket from her. He just stood there as if someone had turned him to stone. His brilliant eyes gleamed from between the dark lashes and his golden skin suddenly seemed taut over his cheekbones. 'You know, you're really going to have to stop doing this, Amber,' he said softly. 'I've given you several chances but my patience is wearing thin and, in the end, I'm only made out of flesh and blood—the same as any other man.'

'What are you talking about?'

'Oh, come on.' His voice was edged with a note of irritation. 'There are many parts you play exceedingly well, but innocence isn't one of them. Much more of those big green eyes gazing at me like that and licking at your lips like a cat which has just seen a mouse—and I'll be forced to kiss you, whether I want to or not.'

Amber looked at him, genuinely confused. 'Why would you even consider kissing me if you didn't want to?'

He laughed, but his laugh contained something dark and unknown and Amber felt as if she were a non-swimmer paddling on the edge of the shore, not noticing the powerful tug of the undercurrent edging towards her.

'Because you're not my kind of woman and because I am, in effect, your employer.' His voice dipped to a silken whisper. 'But that doesn't mean I don't want to.'

His unmistakable passion mixed with the complexity of her own feelings filled Amber with a sudden sense of power and she tilted her chin to look at him defiantly. 'Well, if you really want to kiss me that badly, why don't you just go ahead and do it?'

'I don't kiss women who smoke.'

There was a pause. 'But I haven't had a cigarette since that day I came to your office.'

'You haven't?' His eyes narrowed. 'Why not?'

Should she tell him the truth? Because he'd told her she smelt disgusting and had made her feel *dirty*. But mainly because she'd wanted to show him she could. Somehow Conall Devlin had succeeded where two very expensive hypnotherapy courses had failed, and she'd quit smoking without a single craving.

'Because I am at heart a very obedient woman.' Shamelessly she batted her eyelashes at him. 'Didn't you know that?'

It was provocation pure and simple and Conall felt something inside him snap, like a piece of elastic which had been stretched beyond endurance. He heard the roar of blood in his ears and felt the jerk of an erection pushing hard against his jeans as he found himself pulling her into his arms and breathing in her warmth.

'The only thing I know is that you are a stubborn and defiant woman who has tested me beyond endurance,' he said, his voice rough. 'And maybe this has been inevitable all along.'

She stared into his eyes. 'You're going to put me across your lap and smack my bottom?'

'Is that what you'd like? Maybe later. But not right now. Right now I'm going to kiss you—but be warned that this is going to spoil you for anyone else. Are you prepared for that, Amber? That every man who kisses you after this is going to make you remember me and ache for me?'

'You are *so* arrogant,' she accused.

But her lips were parting and Conall knew she wanted this just as much as him. Maybe more—for he caught a flash of hunger in her darkening eyes. Sliding one hand around her waist while the other cushioned her still-damp hair, he lowered his mouth onto hers. And didn't part of him *want* her to have lied to him—to discover the stale odour of tobacco on those soft lips so that he could pull away in disgust?

But she hadn't lied. She tasted of peppermint and she smelt of daisies and the way she melted into his body was like throwing a match onto a pile of bone-dry timber. He groaned as he felt the stony stud of her nipples pressing against him and he reached down to cup one between his thumb and forefinger, enjoying the way she squirmed beneath his touch and whispered his name. He was so hard that he was afraid that his jeans might rip open all by themselves and, with something which sounded like a roar, he pushed her against the open door, so that it rocked crazily beneath the sudden urgent force of their bodies.

They kissed as if they'd just discovered how to kiss. Her arms were reaching up to his shoulders, as if she was trying to stop herself from sliding to the ground, and as Conall nudged his thigh between hers he was tempted to do just that. To lay her down on the hard floorboards and rip off their clothes and just *take* her, as he had been wanting to for days. Because if he did that—wouldn't he rid his blood of this fever so that he could just *forget* her? His hand cupped her breast and she gasped, drawing in a shuddering breath as he bent his head and grazed his teeth against the nipple which was hard against her damp silk shirt.

'C-Conall,' she gasped.

'I know,' he ground out as desire shot through him in a potent stream. 'Good, isn't it?' With his middle finger, he rubbed along the seam of her jeans at the crotch and he could feel her heat searing through the thick denim as she wriggled her hips in silent invitation.

The scent of sex and of desire was as potent as any perfume and he groped his hand downwards, reaching for his belt. He tugged it open and was just about to undo the top button of his jeans when some sharp splinter of sanity lanced into his thoughts and reality hit him like a slug to the jaw. He dragged his lips away, his eyes focusing and then refocusing as he stared at her and took a step back. Her shirt was half-open and her magnificent breasts were rising and falling as she struggled to control her breathing. Her black hair was plastered to her head, her eyes streaked with mascara from the rain and her lips were rosy-pink and trembling. He wondered what part of teaching her how to try to be a better person this fell under and a wave of self-disgust shot through him as he thought of what he'd just done. And what he'd been tempted to do…

Since when did he violate another man's trust in him, when he knew all too well how painful the consequences of shattered trust could be?

And since when did he lose control like that?

'Is something…wrong?' she questioned.

But he didn't answer. He was too angry with himself to even try. Did she put out like that for everyone? he wondered furiously. Was he just one in a long line of men she indiscriminately chose to satisfy her sexual needs? He took another step away from her, even though every sinew of his body was screaming out its protest. And yes, at that moment he would have traded his entire fortune to slide her panties down her legs and unzip himself and take her, but some last shred of reason stopped him as he reminded himself of the stark reality. That she was everything he'd spent his life trying to avoid and that wasn't about to change any time soon.

It was difficult to speak when all he could think about was thrusting deep into her and losing himself inside her. Difficult to regain control when his heart was racing so hard that it hurt, but Conall had learnt many lessons in his life and masking his temper had been right at the top of the list. He hid it now, replacing it with a silky reason which was always effective.

'Oh, Amber.' Slowly he shook his head. 'Where did you learn to look at a man like that and make him want to go against everything he believes in?'

Her expression was dazed but for once she

wasn't flying back at him with one of her smart comments and that pleased him, for it gave him back the power which had momentarily deserted him.

'Judging by the look on your face and your body language, I imagine you must be greedily anticipating the next time,' he continued, struggling to control his ragged breathing. 'But I'm afraid there isn't going to be one. Because that was something which should never have happened. Do you understand what I'm saying, Amber? From now on we're going to stick to business and only business—so be downstairs at the time I told you so that I can brief you before the Prince arrives.' His mouth hardened into a grim and resolute line. 'And we'll both forget this ever happened.'

CHAPTER SIX

AMBER'S HANDS WERE trembling as she shut
the door on Conall and tried to block out the
sounds of his retreating footsteps—but it
wasn't so easy to blot out the mocking words
which still echoed around her head.

Forget it had ever happened?

Was he out of his *mind*?

Her fingers strayed to lips which felt as if
they were on fire—as if he'd branded them
with that hot and hungry kiss. Leaning back
against the door, she closed her eyes. He'd
done things to her she shouldn't have allowed
him to do. He'd touched her breasts and put
his hand in between her legs but instead of
feeling outrage or disgust—or even her ha-
bitual freezing fear—she had embraced every
moment of it. It had been the most erotic thing
which had ever happened to her until he had
ended it so abruptly. His belt undone, he had

pulled away from her with disgust darkening his eyes, his accusatory words making her sound like some sort of predator—as if she were using all her wiles to lure him into her bed. Oh, the irony.

Walking over to the window, she stared out over the beautiful green parkland and thought about the way she'd responded to him. How *infuriating* that a desire which had eluded her all these years had been awoken by a man who made no secret of despising her. Who had looked at her as if she were something he'd discovered in a dark corner of a room and wished he hadn't. And his rejection had hurt. Of course it had—especially coming so fast on the heels of the nice things he'd said about her painting.

What mattered now was how she reacted to it. Why take all the responsibility for something *he* had started? Why not show Conall Devlin just what she was capable of? Show him that she was not going to become some simpering fangirl, but do what she had been brought down here to do.

Quickly she unpacked her case and took a shower—and afterwards studied the couple of dresses she'd brought with her, realising that Conall had only ever seen her in a series of unflattering outfits. She brushed her fingertips over the soft fabrics, unsure which one to pick. The scarlet was more show-stopping and did wonders for her silhouette—but something stopped her from choosing it. Instead she pulled the ivory silk chiffon from one of the hangers and gave a small smile. She might have rejected most of the rules of her upbringing, but she could still remember what they were. That less was more and quality counted—especially if you were dealing with a royal prince.

By six-thirty, and feeling more confident, she was swishing her way down the sweeping staircase into the entrance hall, where the buckets of flowers had been transformed into lavish displays. She could see Conall deep in conversation on his cell phone, but he raised his bent head as Amber reached the bottom of the stairs. His eyes narrowed and she felt a beat of satisfaction as she registered his expression. He looked *amazed*. As if she'd grown a pair of wings in the time it had taken her to get ready and come downstairs. Suddenly she was glad that she'd opted for no jewellery other than a discreet pair of pearl studs at her ears and that her newly washed hair fell simply down over her shoulders.

'Hi, Conall,' she said. 'I do hope I'm appropriately dressed to meet this royal guest of yours.'

Conall didn't often find himself lost for words but right now it was a struggle to know what to say. A raw and visceral reaction began to pound its way through his body as Amber came downstairs. He stared at her with a mixture of anger and desire, feeling his groin begin to inevitably harden beneath the material of his suit trousers. How the hell did she manage to make him *feel* this way— every damned time? As if he would die if he didn't touch her. Unwillingly his gaze drifted over her, lingering in a way he couldn't seem to help. Her dress fell in creamy folds to the ground, beneath which you could just see the peep of a silver shoe. With her black hair a sleek curtain of ebony and her eyes as green as a cat's, she looked…

He swallowed. She looked as if butter wouldn't melt in that hot mouth of hers. Like those girls he used to see when he was growing up and his mother was working at the big house. The kind you were encouraged to look at because they always wanted you to look at them, but were forbidden to touch.

But he was no longer the servant's son who had to accept what he was told, he reminded himself grimly. He was more than Amber Carter's equal—he was her *boss*—and he was the one calling the shots.

'Very presentable,' he answered coolly. 'And certainly an improvement on anything I've seen you wear before.'

She cocked her head to one side. 'Do you always end a compliment with a criticism?'

He shrugged. 'Depends who I'm talking to. I don't think a little criticism would go amiss in your case. But if the point of you coming down here looking like some kind of goddess is to try to snare the Prince, let me save you the trouble by telling you that he has a bona fide princess in the wings who's waiting for him to marry her.'

She shot him an unfriendly look. 'I'm not interested in "snaring" anyone.'

'Even though acquiring a wealthy husband would be a convenient way out of your current financial predicament?'

'Oh, come on! Which century are you living in, Conall? Women don't have to *sell* themselves through marriage any more. They take jobs like this—working for men whose default mechanism is to be moody and more than a little difficult.'

'Or they get Daddy to support them,' he mocked.

'Not any more, it seems,' she said sweetly. 'So why don't we get the show on the road? You're supposed to be giving me a guided tour of the house and showing me this painting the Prince wants to buy.'

Conall nodded as he gestured her to follow him, but he could feel the growing tension in his body as she walked beside him, aware of the filmy material which drifted enticingly against her body and whispered against every luscious curve. Her arms and her neck were the only skin visible and it was difficult to reconcile this almost ethereal image with the earthy woman who had kissed him so fervently in the bedroom earlier.

Tonight his country house looked perfect, like something you might see in the pages of one of those glossy magazines—but hadn't that always been his intention? Wasn't this the pinnacle of a long-held dream—to acquire a stately home even bigger than the one his mother had worked in during his childhood? A way of redressing some sort of balance which had always felt fundamentally skewed.

He led Amber through the ground floor—furnished and recently decorated in the traditional style—showing her the drawing rooms, the library and the grand conservatory. In the ballroom where the party was being held, a string quartet was tuning up and bottles of pink champagne were being put on ice. Everywhere he looked he could see candlelight and the air was scented with the fragrance of cut flowers and the sweet smell of success.

But Conall felt as if he was just going through the motions of showing Amber his home. As though all this lavish wealth suddenly meant nothing. Was that because the beautiful antiques just looked like bog-standard pieces of furniture when compared to the black-haired beauty by his side? Or because all he wanted to do was to drag her off to some dark corner to finish off what he had begun earlier?

He took her to a galleried room at the far end of the house, outside which a burly guard stood. The velvet drapes were drawn against the night outside and on one bare wall—beautifully lit—hung a painting.

'Here it is,' he said.

Amber was glad to have something to concentrate on other than the man at her side, or the remark he'd made earlier about her looking like a goddess. Had he meant it? A wave of impatience swept over her. *Stop reading into his words. Stop imagining he feels anything for you other than lust.*

Stepping back, she began to study the canvas—a luminous portrait of a young woman executed in oils. The woman was wearing a silver headband in her pale bobbed hair and a silver nineteen-twenties flapper dress. It was painted so finely that the subject seemed to be sending out an unspoken message to the onlooker and there was a trace of sadness in her lustrous dark eyes.

'It's exquisite,' Amber said softly.

'I know it is. Utterly exquisite.' He turned to her. 'And you're clear what you need to do? Stay by the Prince's side all evening and speak only when spoken to. Try to refrain from being controversial and please let me know if he communicates any concerns to one of his aides. Think you can manage that?'

'I can try.'

'Good. Then let's go and wait for the guest of honour.'

They walked towards the ballroom, where Amber could hear the string quartet playing a lively piece which floated out to greet them. 'So who else is coming tonight?' she asked.

'Some old friends are coming down from London. A few colleagues from New York. Local people.'

She hesitated. 'Do you ever see my half-brother, Rafe?'

His footsteps slowed and he shook his head. 'Not for ages. Not since he went out to Australia and cut himself off from his old life and nobody knew why.'

Remembering an offhand remark her father had once made, she glanced up at his rugged profile. 'I think it was something to do with a woman.'

'It's always to do with a woman, Amber. Especially when there's trouble.' He turned his head towards her and gave a hard smile. 'What do the French say? *Cherchez la femme.*'

'Is that cynicism I can hear in your voice? Did some girl break your heart, Conall?'

'Not mine, sweetheart. Mine's made of

stone—didn't you know?' His eyes glittered. 'All I heard was that Rafe was heavily disillusioned by some woman and his life was never the same afterwards. It's a lesson for us all.'

He really *was* cynical, thought Amber as he introduced her to the party planner—a freckled redhead who clearly thought Conall was the greatest thing since sliced bread. Along with just about every other female present. Amber wondered if he was oblivious to the way the waitresses looked up and practically melted as they offered their trays of canapés and drinks. Whether he noticed that the female guests were fawning all over him. He *must* do—but, she had to admit, he handled it brilliantly. He was charming but he didn't flirt back—thus risking the wrath of their partners. She watched as he shook hands and made introductions as the room began to fill up, a smile creasing his rugged features.

She moved away, trying to remember that she was here as a member of his staff and not as his guest—wishing that she could retain a little immunity when she was close to him. She found herself a soft drink and stood in an alcove, watching as even more people arrived and the level of chatter increased. There was a discreet buzz of anticipation in the air, as if everyone was waiting for their royal guest, but Amber only became aware of the Prince's arrival when a complete silence suddenly descended on the ballroom.

People instantly parted to create a central path for him and the imposing man who walked in accompanied by two aides was instantly recognisable from the images Amber had downloaded from the Internet. With his immaculately cut dark suit and his golden skin gleaming, he had a charisma which was matched by only one other man in the room, who instantly stepped forward to greet him.

Amber watched as Conall gave a brief bow before shaking Luciano's hand and the string quartet broke into what was obviously the national anthem of Mardovia. And then a pair of midnight eyes were silently seeking her out and she found herself walking towards them, forcing herself to concentrate on the Prince and not on the rugged Irishman who had touched her so intimately.

'Your Royal Highness, this is Amber Carter—one of my assistants. Amber will be on hand tonight to provide anything you should require.'

That horrendous year at finishing school in Switzerland had taught Amber very little other than how to play truant and to ski, but it came up trumps now as she executed a deep and perfect curtsey. She rose slowly to her feet and the Prince smiled.

'Anything?' he drawled, his eyes roving down over her with an appreciative stare.

Amber wondered if she'd imagined Conall's faint frown and imperceptibly she nodded to the hovering waitress. 'Perhaps you would care for something to drink, Your Royal Highness?'

'Certo,' he answered softly in Italian, taking a glass of Kir Royale from the tray and then raising it to her in silent salute.

But Amber found herself enjoying the Prince's unexpected attention. For the first time in a long time she found herself encouraged by the sense that here was something she *could* do. She might not have any real qualifications but she'd watched enough of her father's wives and girlfriends fluttering around to know how *not* to behave if you were trying to play the perfect hostess. Even her mother had been able to pull it out of the bag when the need had arisen.

Unobtrusively she stood by to make sure the Prince wasn't approached by any stray star-struck guests as Conall introduced Luciano to several carefully vetted guests. It seemed he'd recently bought a penthouse apartment through Conall's company and she listened while the two men chatted with a local land-owner about the escalating fortunes of the London property market. More waitresses appeared with tiny caviar-topped canapés but she noticed that the Prince refused them all. Eventually he turned to Conall.

'Do you think I have properly fulfilled my role as guest of honour,' he questioned drily, 'and given this occasion the royal stamp of approval?'

'You'd like to see the painting now?'

'I think you have tantalised me with it for long enough, don't you?'

Conall looked at her. 'Amber?'

She nodded, aware of two bodyguards who had suddenly appeared at the entrance to the ballroom and who now walked behind them towards the gallery. She thought what a disparate group they made as they made their way through the empty corridors.

The guard at the door stepped aside and

Amber watched Luciano's reaction as he stepped forward to stand directly in front of the canvas. She thought that someone trying to negotiate a better price might have feigned a little indifference towards the painting, but the admiration on his face was impossible to conceal.

'What do you think?' asked Conall.

'It is breathtaking,' the Prince said slowly as he leaned forward to study it more closely. He murmured something in Italian to one of his aides and several minutes passed in silence before eventually he turned to Conall. 'We will discuss prices when you are back in London, not tonight. Business should never be distracted by pleasure.'

Conall inclined his head. 'I shall look forward to it.'

'Perhaps you could check that my car is ready? And in the meantime, I really think I must dance with your assistant who has looked after me so well all evening.' The Prince smiled. 'Unless she has any objections?'

The Prince's bright blue eyes were turned in her direction and Amber felt a stab of satisfaction. The Prince of Mardovia had told everyone that she'd done a good job—even though she'd done nothing more onerous than act as his gatekeeper—and now he wanted to dance with her. It was a long time since she could remember feeling this good about herself.

'I'd love to,' she said simply.

'Eccellente.'

She was aware of Conall's fleeting frown before he went to chase up the Prince's transport and aware of the envious glances of the other women in the ballroom as the Prince pulled her into his arms and the string quartet began to play a soft and easy waltz. Amber had been to some flashy parties in her time, but even she knew it wasn't every night of the week that you got to dance with a prince and Luciano ticked all the right boxes. He was supremely handsome and extremely attentive, but the weird thing was that it felt almost like dancing with her *brother*. Innocent and sweet, but almost dutiful. His arms around her waist felt nothing like Conall's had felt when he'd hauled her into his arms earlier. Despite the fact that he'd told her to forget it, she found herself remembering the way he had kissed her. Kissed her so hard that he'd left her feeling dazed.

'Devlin is your lover?' the Prince questioned suddenly, his voice breaking into her thoughts and amplifying them.

Slightly taken aback by his candour, Amber bit her lip. 'No!'

'But he would like to be.'

She shook her head. 'He hates me,' she said without thinking and then remembered that she was supposed to be there in the role of facilitator—not pouring out her heart to a royal stranger. 'I'm sorry—'

But Luciano didn't seem to notice for he lifted his hand to silence her apology. 'He may hate you, but he wants you. He watches you as the snake watches a chicken, just before it devours it whole.'

Amber shivered. 'That's not a very nice image to paint, Your Highness.'

'Maybe not, but it is an accurate one.' He gave her a cool smile. 'And you really should have mentioned that you speak Italian.'

Amber could feel a hot blush rising in her cheeks, so that any thought of denying it went straight out of the window. She looked up into Luciano's bright blue eyes. 'How—?'

'Not difficult.' He smiled. 'When I was speaking to my aide you were trying very hard not to react to what I was saying, but I am adept in observing reactions. I have had enough attempts made on my life to recognise subterfuge, even though I sometimes cannot help but admire it. Tell Conall I had always intended to give him a fair price for the painting.'

Amber tilted her chin. 'She's related to you, isn't she? The woman in the painting?'

He grew still. 'You recognised the family likeness, even though our colouring is quite different?'

Amber nodded. 'I'm…I'm quite good at doing that. I have a lot of half-brothers and sisters.'

'She is the daughter of my great-grandfather's brother who was born at the beginning of the last century. He fell in love with an Englishwoman and eloped with her to America. It caused a great scandal in Mardovia at the time.'

'I can imagine,' commented Amber.

Luciano glanced at his watch. 'At any other time I would be fascinated to continue this discussion but look over there—the Irishman has returned and his expression tells me that he does not like to see you in my arms like this.'

'And you care what he thinks?'

'No, but I think you do.'

Amber stiffened. 'Maybe I do,' she admitted.

Luciano's eyes narrowed as he swung her round with a flourish, to the final few bars of the music. 'You are not aware of his reputation, I think?'

'With women?'

'With women, yes. And with business,' he commented drily. 'He is known for a detachment and a ruthlessness he has demonstrated tonight by placing a *spy* in my camp.'

Amber felt her cheeks grow pink. Hadn't she accused him of the very same thing? 'I'm sure that wasn't his intention at all,' she said doggedly.

The Prince smiled. 'Ah! Your loyalty to the man is touching—but do not look so alarmed, Amber. Conall and I know one another of old and I have great admiration for someone as ruthless as I am—but I would heed any sensible woman to exercise caution with such a man.'

Amber's cheeks were still burning as the Prince dropped his hands from her waist as Conall returned to escort him to his waiting car.

There was a loud buzz of chatter as the royal party left the room and Amber moved away from the dance floor and went to stand by the cool shelter of a marble pillar. With both men gone she felt like Cinderella—as if she no longer had any right to be here. As if any minute now her beautiful cream dress would turn into rags. She looked around. Maybe she should take the opportunity to slip out of the ballroom and go back to her room before Conall came back. Nobody would miss her. He might even be glad that she was out of his hair and he could party on without compunction.

But suddenly the decision was taken out of her hands because Conall had returned and was standing in the entrance to the ballroom, his dark suit hugging his muscular frame. He had undone a couple of buttons of his white silk shirt and Amber could see the faint smattering of dark hair there.

His eyes searched the room until he'd found her and as he began to walk towards her, her heart began to pound painfully in her chest. Would he be angry with her? She might have rather clumsily allowed the Prince to realise she was a linguist but he hadn't seemed to mind and she had done her best. Surely even Conall could understand that.

He was standing in front of her now, his

midnight eyes shuttered. He didn't say a single word, just took her hand and led her onto the dance floor and Amber could feel her pulse rocketing skywards as he pulled her into his arms.

'Wh-what are you doing?' she questioned shakily, because she hadn't felt remotely like this when she'd been dancing with Luciano.

'Taking over where the Prince left off.' His eyes gleamed. 'Unless you have decided that dancing with mere mortals has no appeal compared to the heady delights of having a blue-blooded partner?'

'Don't be ridiculous,' she said. 'I'm quite happy to dance with you as long as you promise not to tread on my foot.'

His hands tightened around her waist. 'And that's your only stipulation, is it, Amber?'

Her eyes were fixed on the sprinkling of chest hair which was now exactly at eye level. 'I could think of plenty more.'

'Such as?'

'I wonder why you want to dance with me when you seem to have been glaring at me all evening.'

'Is that what I've been doing?'

'You know you have. Is it…' She hesitated.

'Is it because the Prince guessed that I spoke Italian?'

He laughed. 'He said you frowned when he used the word assassination. I guess most people would. And no, it's not because of that.'

'What, then?'

His hands tightened around her waist. 'Maybe because I have conflicting feelings about you.'

She lifted her face up and met the hard gleam of his eyes. He had *feelings* for her? She could do absolutely nothing about the sudden race of her heart—only pray he couldn't detect its erratic thumping. 'What do you mean?'

Idly, he began to rub his thumb up and down over her ribcage. 'Just that you arouse me. Deeply and constantly. And I can't seem to get you out of my mind.'

If anyone else had come out and said that Amber would have been shocked or scared, but somehow when Conall said it she was neither. 'And I'm supposed to be flattered by such a statement?'

'I don't know,' he said simply. 'My biggest concern is what I'm going to do about it.'

She could feel danger whispering in the air around them, but far more potent was the sense of excitement which made the danger easy to ignore. 'And the options are?'

'Don't be disingenuous, Amber, because it doesn't suit you.' Almost experimentally, he rolled his thumb over one of her ribs, slowly rubbing along the chiffon-covered bone. 'You know very well what the options are. I can take you upstairs so that we can finish off what we started earlier and maybe rid myself of this damned fever which has been raging in my blood since the moment I first saw you draped all over that white leather sofa.'

Somehow Amber stopped herself from reacting. Since *then*? 'Or?'

'Or I trawl this ballroom looking for someone who would make a more suitable bed partner on so many levels.' His voice dipped to a deep caress so that it sounded like velvet brushing over gravel. 'There's a third choice, of course—but not nearly so inviting. Because I could always go and take a long, cold shower and steer clear of all the complications of sex.'

Amber said nothing. He'd made her sound as disposable as a paper handkerchief. As forgettable as last night's tangled dreams. Yet he wasn't lying to her, was he? He wasn't dressing up his desire with fancy words and meaningless phrases—raising up her hopes before smashing them down again. He wasn't promising her the stars, but his underlying message was that he would deliver on satisfaction. And didn't she want that satisfaction for the first time in her life? Didn't she want to sample what other women just took for granted?

She thought about what the Prince had said to her. That a sensible woman would exercise caution. She guessed he'd been warning her off Conall Devlin, for whatever reason. But she wasn't known for being *sensible*, was she? She was known as a wild child—the party animal who was up for anything. And only she knew the truth—that all her wildness was nothing but a façade behind which she hid, a barrier which nobody had ever been able to break down.

But Conall Devlin had got closer than anyone else.

She closed her eyes as she felt his fingers pressing against her flesh and she was acutely conscious that they were inches away from her breast. Through the delicate fabric of her silk dress it felt as if he were touching her bare skin and she felt a shiver rippling down her spine. How did he *do* that? What power did he have which made her respond to him like this and make her so achingly aware of her own body? The hard jut of his hips and the potent cradle of his masculinity as he pressed himself closer should have intimidated a woman of her laughable experience, but it didn't. It just made her want more. Much more. Was she really prepared to turn her back on this opportunity to become a real woman at last?

Instinct made her lips part as she looked into his eyes and saw the sudden gleam of intensity in his darkened gaze.

'And don't I get a say in what happens?' she questioned, as lightly as if she had this kind of conversation every day of the week.

'Of course. You get to choose—because that is a woman's prerogative. Tell me what *you* want, Amber.'

The mood of the conversation had switched and beneath the teasing banter of his tone she could sense his sudden urgency. But still Amber held back, telling herself to confront the reality of what was happening here. For him this was just a liaison no different from countless others—apart from her name and her hair colour, she was probably as interchangeable as the last woman who had shared his bed.

And for her?

It was going to be no good if she started weakening. If she made the mistake of falling for him. She could only go ahead if she accepted it for what it was. Not stardust and roses, but a powerful sexual hunger. A physical awakening which was long overdue.

Rising up on tiptoe, she put her lips to his ear and only just refrained from sliding her tongue across the lobe.

'I want to have sex with you,' she whispered.

Conall stiffened, thinking he had misheard her. He must have done. She had been feisty and defiant every step of the way—surely she wasn't rolling over and capitulating *that* easily. And didn't he *want* her to go on resisting him for a little while longer, because it was so deliciously rare and because the conquest was never quite as good as the chase...

'You mean that?' he questioned softly, his fingertips continuing to slide over her silk-covered torso.

She nodded, her words uncharacteristically brief. 'Yes. Yes, I do.'

A smile curved the edges of his lips as he felt the heat begin to rise within him. 'Very well. This is what I want you to do. You will go upstairs to your room and wait for me while I say goodbye to my guests. But you will not undress before I arrive.' He paused. 'Because undressing a woman is one of the greatest pleasures known to man. Is that clear?'

She nodded—more obedient than he had ever seen her. 'Very clear.'

'I shall come to you before midnight.' He tilted her chin with his thumb and stared straight into her emerald eyes. 'But if before that you decide—for whatever reason—that you've changed your mind, then you must tell me and we will consider this conversation never to have happened. Do you understand?'

'Yes, Conall.'

He put his lips very close to her ear. 'I'm not quite sure how to cope with this unusually docile Amber.'

She turned her head to meet his gaze. 'Would you prefer defiance, then?'

'I'll let you know in graphic detail exactly what I'd prefer but I think it had better wait until we are alone. Because my words are having an unfortunate but predictable effect on my body, and having you this close to me is making me want to tear that dress off you and see the flesh beneath, and I don't think that would go down very well with my guests, do you?'

She shook her head but, to his surprise, her cheeks flushed a deep shade of pink and he felt a doubling of his desire for her. 'Go upstairs and wait for me,' he said roughly. 'Because the sooner this evening ends, the sooner we can begin.'

CHAPTER SEVEN

AMBER HEARD A CREAK behind her and turned to see the handle turning and the door slowly opening to reveal Conall standing rock still on the threshold of her bedroom. The light from the corridor spilled in from behind him, turning his muscular physique into a powerful silhouette, but not for long—because he closed the door and walked across the room, his eyes shuttered as he grew close and looked down at her. His voice sounded like velvet encasing steel.

'Changed your mind?'

She shook her head. Admittedly, she *had* been having second thoughts about their cold-blooded sexual liaison as she'd been sitting perched on the window seat waiting for him. Not undressing as per his curt instructions and feeling a bit like a sacrificial lamb in her evening dress as she stared out at the bright stars which spattered the night sky and the crescent moon which gleamed against the darkness. But her flutterings of apprehension were nothing compared to the stealthy creep of desire which was making her nerve endings feel so raw and her breasts so heavy and tingling. 'No,' she said unsteadily. 'I haven't changed my mind.'

Conall expelled the breath he hadn't realised he'd been holding because hadn't he almost wished she *had*? He'd been plagued by feelings of guilt the moment she had walked off the dance floor with her pale dress floating around her like a cloud. He had felt tortured by his conscience and even now something told him he should get out while he still could.

'I told your father that I would set you on the right path,' he growled.

She looked up into his face. 'And you have. You know you have. I felt so confident tonight—as if anything was possible and it was because of you and the chance you gave me. A few weeks ago I wouldn't have done that but you've made me see new possibilities. I'm a grown woman, Conall, not a child—so don't treat me like one. And my father is not my keeper.'

Transfixed by the unusually steadfast note in her voice and the rise and fall of her breasts, Conall felt the last of his resistance melting away as he took hold of her hands and lifted her to her feet. In the moonlight her face was almost as pale as her silky dress and, in vivid contrast, her dark hair spilled like ebony over her shoulders. She looked like a witch, he thought longingly. *Was* she a witch? Able to enchant him with things he suspected were the wrong things for a man like him? His mouth hardened. *So make sure she knows your boundaries. Make sure she doesn't read anything into what is going to happen.*

'I guess we'd better have the disclaimer conversation,' he said abruptly.

She blinked up at him. 'Disclaimer conversation?'

'Sure. I'm pretty certain a hard-partying woman like you isn't going to object to a one-night stand on moral grounds but just in case—I'd better make it clear that this is all this is going to be. One night. Great sex. But no more.' He raised his eyebrows. 'Any objections?'

'None from me,' she said, in that flippant way which was so much a part of her, though for a second he wondered if he had imagined the faint shadow which crossed over her face. 'So what are we waiting for?'

Heart pounding, he reached for the zip of her dress and slid it down. One small tug and it had pooled to her ankles and she was standing wearing nothing but her high-heeled silver shoes and her underwear.

Conall frowned because somehow her lingerie didn't match her sassy image. Her plain white bra looked like something a woman might wear to the gym and she had on a pair of those big knickers which had been the butt of a national joke for a while. It was not the lingerie of a woman who had boldly whispered to him on the dance floor that she wanted to have sex with him and that puzzled him.

Had she sensed his disquiet? Was that why she reached behind her and unclipped her bra—as careless as a woman getting changed on the beach? He stilled as her breasts spilled free and he felt a jerk of almost unbearable lust as he stared at them. Did she know that they were the stuff of his fevered fantasies—large yet pert, with their rosy-pink and perfect nipples? Of course she did. With a groan he pulled her into his arms and pushed back the spill of her hair as he kissed her. He kissed her until she was melting and her lips opened eagerly beneath his, until she began to move restlessly in his arms. And when he drew his face away, her eyes looked huge and dark in her face. As if she was completely dazed by that kiss. Conall shook his head a little. Come to think of it—wasn't he a little dazed himself?

'You are the most unfathomable woman I've ever met, Amber Carter,' he groaned, taking each nipple between a finger and a thumb and squeezing them until she squirmed with pleasure.

Her eyelids seemed to be having difficulty staying open. 'And is that a good thing, or a bad thing?'

'I haven't made my mind up yet. It's unusual, that's for sure.' He leaned forward and brushed his lips over hers. 'I keep thinking I've got you all worked out and then you go and confound all my expectations.'

'And what do you have me worked out as?'

He laughed and his voice grew serious as he traced the outline of her lips with his finger. 'One minute you're unbearably spoilt, with a sense of entitlement so strong it almost takes my breath away, while the next...'

But Amber halted his words by leaning forward to kiss him, mimicking the almost careless way he'd just brushed his lips over hers. She guessed what was coming and she didn't want to hear it. She didn't dare. She didn't want to hear about her flaws and she certainly didn't want him to work out why she was feeling out of her depth. He was a sexually experienced man—and a perceptive man—who was doubtless going to make some comment about her seeming gauche and innocent. Some bone-deep instinct told her he would run a mile if he knew the truth—and that was something she wasn't prepared to tolerate. Because she wanted Conall Devlin. She didn't care if it was a one-night stand. She couldn't think beyond the sudden urgent needs of her body and she wanted him more than she could remember wanting anything. More than the security she'd prayed for as a child, or the peace which had always eluded her. More than any of that.

So stop behaving like someone who is a stranger to intimacy. Start being the person he thinks you are.

Looping her arms around his neck, she

slanted him a coquettish smile. 'Look, I know the Irish are famous for talking, but do you think we could save this conversation until later?'

And suddenly they seemed to be reading from the same page, because his eyes gleamed. 'Oh, I'm happy to skip the talking, sweetheart,' he promised, his voice laden with silken intent. 'What is it they say—action, not words?'

He picked her up and carried her over to the four-poster bed, laying her down on top of it and bending his head to a nipple. Her eyes closed as his tongue flicked over the puckered skin and his teeth gently grazed the engorged nub, making her wriggle her hips with helpless pleasure before he turned his attention to the other. Sweet sensation speared through her, flooding her body with a sudden rush of honeyed warmth as his dark head moved over her sensitive skin. Did he realise that her desire was rapidly building, or could he detect it from the subtle new perfume now scenting the air? Was that why he slipped his hand between her legs, burrowing beneath the plain white fabric of her briefs and brushing over the mound of curls before alighting on the heated flesh beneath?

She felt so wet. Maybe that was why he gave a low laugh which sent shivers down her spine. Amber's mouth dried as he began to move his finger against her so that her little gasp was scarcely more than a sigh. It felt as if he were building a wall of pleasure, brick by delicious brick, and she fell back against the pillows, her thighs parting of their own accord, when suddenly he stopped. Her eyes snapped open, terrified he had changed his mind. Her heart pounded. *He mustn't change his mind!*

But he was smiling as he shook his head. 'No,' he said. 'Not like that. Not the first time.'

He moved away from the bed and began to undress—removing his clothes and producing a small silver packet from his pocket with an efficiency which suggested he'd done this many times before. Of course he had. And although fear that she would somehow disappoint him began to bubble up inside her—it quickly disappeared the moment she saw him in all his naked glory.

Amber shivered. He was like a classical statue you might see in a museum—with broad shoulders tapering down to narrow hips and muscular legs. But statues didn't have tawny skin which glowed with life, nor midnight eyes which gleamed with hunger. Inevitably, her gaze was drawn down towards the cradle of his masculinity where, against a palette of jet-dark curls, his erection was thick and pale and prominent. Amber felt her pulse go shooting skywards. She'd never got this far before—she'd always fallen at much earlier hurdles—and perhaps she should have been daunted by what she saw. But she wasn't. It felt natural. As if it was supposed to happen. As if fate had intended it to happen—before she reminded herself that she wasn't going down that path. Stardust and roses weren't part of this equation, she reminded herself fiercely. This was sex. Nothing but sex. He'd told her that himself.

'I like it,' he murmured as he came over to the bed and pulled her into his arms.

'Wh-what?'

'The look on your face.' He smiled. 'As if this was the first time all over again. Have you spent years perfecting that look of wonder and innocence, Amber—knowing just how much it will turn a man on?'

If she'd written the script herself, there

wouldn't have been a better time to tell him but Amber couldn't bring herself to say it. Because now he was kissing her and his hands were starfishing over her breasts and she could feel his hardness pressing against her belly.

'Conall,' she gasped as he pulled back for a moment to slide her panties down and she lifted up her bottom to help him.

'You were the one who didn't want to talk,' he murmured as he fumbled for the silver packet he'd put beside the bed. 'Though maybe you'd better say something to distract me because I've never had so much trouble putting on a damned condom.'

'Be...be careful.'

The smile on his lips died. 'Oh, don't worry, sweetheart. Having a baby with you was never part of my agenda.'

The stark statement was oddly painful and yet somehow it helped. It helped her focus on the way he was making her *feel* and not the conflicting thoughts which were swirling around inside her head.

So she kissed him back with a passion which came from somewhere deep inside her, and with growing confidence began to explore the warm satin of his skin with her mouth and her fingers. And when he moved over her and parted her thighs, the fear she felt was only fleeting. She was twenty-four years old, for heaven's sake. It was time.

Conall gave a groan as he thrust into her, knowing he was going to have to be very careful because he was so aroused he wanted to come straight away. And she was so *tight*. His heart pounded like some caged animal locked inside his chest. Too tight. He gave a near-silent curse as realisation dawned on him and his body stilled. For a moment he almost achieved the impossible by starting to withdraw from her, but the moment was lost the second she cried out and he couldn't work out if the sound was pain or pleasure. Had he hurt her? He stared down into her face, into eyes which were wide—as if seeking some kind of approval—and instantly he shut his own with grim deliberation, not wanting her to see his anger or his disbelief as he began to move inside her. Part of him wanted to just spill his seed and have done with it, but the pride he took in his reputation as a lover made him take his time...

Duplicitous little *bitch*, he thought as he drove into her—each thrust making her gasp out her pleasure. With almost cold-hearted precision he did all the things to her which women liked best. He tilted up her hips to increase the level of penetration while he played with her clitoris. He rode her hard and he rode her slow, and only when he felt her body begin to tense did he let go—and then it was *his* time for bewilderment. Because it had never happened to him before. Not like this. Not at exactly the same time—as if they'd worked very hard at sexual choreography classes to ensure the ultimate in mutual fulfilment. So that as her back began to arch and her long legs began to splay, he couldn't even watch her—he was too busy focusing on his own orgasm, which was welling up inside him like an almighty wave, before taking him under.

Had he thought that the chase was always more tantalising than the conquest? He had been wrong.

Because all he was aware of was the convulsive jerk of his body and the molten rush of heat. Of the sweetest pleasure he had ever known flooding him…and his shuddered cry drowning out the distant hoot of the night owl.

CHAPTER EIGHT

'You acted...'

Conall's words trailed off and Amber didn't prompt him. She didn't want to talk and she didn't want to hear what he had to say. She didn't want to do anything except lie here and go over what had just happened, second by glorious second. To remember the way he'd kissed her. The way he'd pushed deep inside her—and then the growing awareness of her body's reaction, which had seemed too good to be true. Only it hadn't been. It had been very real and very true. Conall Devlin had made love to her and it had been perfect. She expelled a long, slow breath of satisfaction. Suddenly she could understand all the fuss and hype and everything which went with it. Sex was pretty potent stuff.

But then when it was over, he had withdrawn from her without even looking at her.

He had just rolled over onto his back and lain there staring at the ceiling in complete silence. As if he was working out what he was going to say, and something told her she wasn't going to like it...

She was right.

'You acted like you'd been round the block a few times—and then some,' he accused.

She risked a glance at him then and almost wished she hadn't because it triggered off a craving to touch him again and that was the last thing he wanted, judging from the stony look on his face. *You haven't done anything wrong*, she told herself. *And he can only make you feel bad about yourself if you let him.*

'You're objecting to the fact I was a virgin?' she questioned, in a voice which was surprisingly calm. Maybe it was the endorphins rushing through her bloodstream which were responsible—making her feel as if she were floating in the sea, in bright sunshine. 'And you're objecting to the fact that I hadn't *been around the block*, is that what you're saying?'

He turned to look at her, his eyes gleaming in his tawny skin. 'What do you think? You knew what the deal was, Amber.'

'Deal?' she echoed. She raised her eyebrows. 'What deal was that?'

'I told you it was a one-night stand!' he exploded.

'And virgins aren't allowed to have one-night stands?'

'Yes. No! Stop wilfully misunderstanding me!'

'I'm confused, Conall. You still haven't told me why you're so angry.'

He glared at her. 'You know damned well why.'

'No, I don't.'

'There's an unspoken rule about sex—that if you're inexperienced, you tell the man.'

'Why? So that you could be "gentle" with me?'

'So that I could have turned around and walked right out again.'

'Because you didn't want me?'

Conall steeled himself against that uncertain note in her voice, reminding himself that she was a consummate actress. She'd played the vamp to an astonishingly successful degree and had fooled him completely. He'd fantasised about all the sexual tricks she might have learnt over the years. He'd been expecting accomplishment and slickness—not for her to cry out like that when he tore through her hymen. Or to clutch at him like a child with a new toy when he was deep inside her. That wonder on her face had not been feigned, he realised grimly.

'You know I wanted you. My body is programmed to want you. It's a reaction outside my control.'

'Gee. Thanks.'

He shook his head. 'The first time is supposed to be special. It's supposed to *mean* something and if I'd realised, I would have done the decent thing and walked away. But you weren't prepared to let that happen, were you, Amber? You saw something and you just went right ahead and took it because that's the kind of woman you are. Even though you must have known it would never have happened if I'd realised you were a virgin. But Amber always gets what Amber wants, doesn't she?'

'If that's what you want to think, then think it,' she said.

'I just don't understand why.' He frowned. 'How come someone who looks like you and acts like you has never actually had sex before now?'

Amber met the anger in his eyes and wondered how much to tell him. But what was the point in holding back—in trying to pretend that she was a normal woman who'd led a normal life?

'Because I don't really like men,' she said slowly. 'And I certainly don't trust them.'

'Which is why you put out for someone you only met a couple of weeks ago, who hasn't even taken you out on a date?'

Put like that, it made her sound plain stupid. As if she'd been caught scraping the very bottom of the barrel. Amber felt her cheeks growing hot, but she could hardly blame him for speaking the truth—even if it made her feel bad. And was she really going to let him take the moral high ground, just because she hadn't given some embarrassingly graphic explanation before he'd made love to her? Why *would* she ruin the mood and risk spoiling something which had felt so natural?

'I'm sure your colossal ego doesn't need me to tell you why I succumbed to you. You must realise that you're overwhelmingly attractive to women, Conall. I'm sure you've heard it many times before. It must be that blend of Irish charm coupled with a masterful certainty that you always know best.' She snuggled down a little further into the bedclothes, but her skin still felt like ice. 'It must be great to have that kind of unshakeable confidence.'

'We were talking about you, not me,' he growled. 'And you still haven't given me an explanation.'

'Do I have to?'

'Don't you think you owe me one?'

'I don't owe you anything.'

'Okay, then. How about as a favour to me for having given you so much pleasure in the last hour?'

Amber swallowed as she met the arrogant glitter in his eyes. In a way it was easier when he was being hateful because at least that stopped her from fostering any dreamy illusions about him. And she realised that this was the other side of intimacy—not the sex part but the bit where two people were naked in more ways than one. Because for once she couldn't run or hide from the truth. She felt exposed; vulnerable. Conall was demanding an explanation and in her heart she guessed she owed him one.

'Maybe it's because I didn't have the best role models in the world,' she said.

'You're talking about your father?' he questioned curiously.

'Not just my father. There were plenty of others. My mother's lovers, for starters.'

'There were a lot?'

'Oh, yes—you could say that.' She gave a hollow laugh. 'After my parents split, my father gave my mother loads of alimony—I think he was trying to ease his conscience about falling in love with a new woman. With hindsight it was probably a big mistake—because money buys you plenty of things, but not happiness. The biggest cliché in the world, I know, but true.' Amber was aware of the irony of her words. As if it had taken this to make her see things clearly. Because hadn't she experienced the closest thing she'd felt to joy in a long time when she'd been walking in that country lane that afternoon? And then just a few minutes ago, when Conall's naked skin had touched hers and he'd taken her to heaven and back? Only one of those things had cost her…and it couldn't be measured in monetary terms.

'So what happened?' he asked, his deep Irish voice penetrating her thoughts.

'My mother couldn't face staying in England with the humiliation of being replaced by wife number four, who was much younger—as well as being a lingerie model. So she decided to do an extensive tour of Europe—which translated into an extensive tour of European men. The trouble was that she was divorced and predatory, with a child in tow. Not the best combination to help her in her ardent pursuit of a new partner.' She shifted her legs beneath the duvet, taking care to keep them well away from his. 'Oh, there were plenty of men—but the men always seemed to come with baggage, usually in the shape of a wife. We were hounded out of Rome, and Athens, too. We were threatened in Naples and had to slip away in the dead of night. Only in Paris did she achieve any kind of acceptance because there the role of mistress is more or less accepted. Only she didn't like playing second fiddle to other men's wives, and…' Her words tailed off.

'And what?'

A wave of indignation swept over her as she met the hard glitter of his sapphire eyes. Why was he doing this? Interrogating her like some second-rate cop. Was he determined to ruin the amazing memory of what had just happened between them by making her retrace a past it was painful to revisit?

'I'm waiting, Amber,' he said softly.

Stubborn, hateful man. Amber stared straight up at the ceiling. 'I don't want to talk about it,' she said woodenly. 'She died, okay? I was brought back to England, kicking and screaming, and moved in with my father, who by that time was on wife number five. I didn't fit in anywhere—and I knew his latest wife didn't want me there. To him, I was a problem he didn't know how to cope with, so he just threw lots of money at it. I started doing loads of courses but only the ones he thought were suitable and, of course, I never saw them through. I didn't know how to deal with normal life—and I'd known so many creepy men when I was growing up that I simply wasn't interested in getting intimate with any of my own.'

'I see.'

Amber pulled the duvet right up to her neck—noticing he didn't object—before rolling on her side to face him. 'And what *do* you see, Conall?'

He gave a short laugh. 'I can see now why your father was so determined he help you escape from the rut you were in. I detected a sense of remorse in his attitude—a sense that he wanted to try to repair some of the mistakes he'd made in the past. He must have realised that giving you money was having precisely the wrong effect, and that's why he withdrew your funds.'

'Wow. You should be a detective!'

'But you didn't like being broke, did you, Amber?' he continued silkily. 'You didn't like having to knuckle down and do a hard day's work like the rest of the human race.'

'I thought I did a good job for you tonight with the Prince!' she defended, stung.

He nodded reluctantly. 'Oh, you did,' he said. 'He was very impressed with you and who wouldn't be, with your classy dress and your pearls? And, of course, the fact that you were gazing up at him on the dance floor and batting those witchy green eyes certainly didn't do you any harm. But I guess you quickly discovered that he wasn't interested in you and so that quicksilver mind of yours had to come up with an alternative plan.'

'Really? And what *plan* was this, Conall? Do enlighten me—this is absolutely fascinating.'

'I think I can understand why you were a virgin,' he said slowly. 'With a mother who was sexually voracious, you must have realised that virginity is the most prized gift a woman can offer a man. It's unique. A one-off.'

'You've lost me now,' she said faintly.

'Think about it. Because despite your lack of qualifications, you're a super-sharp woman, Amber. You know damned well what I'm talking about. You played the vamp with me. You realised there was real chemistry between us and that all I wanted was casual sex. It was a grown-up agreement between two consenting adults when suddenly you spring this surprise on me. You're a virgin! Though when I stop to think about it, maybe it isn't so surprising after all.' He gave a short laugh. 'Take a previously wealthy woman with nothing to offer but her innocence—and throw her into the arms of an old-fashioned man with a conscience and the result is predictable.'

'What *result*?'

Despite their cold hue, his eyes suddenly looked as if they were capable of scorching her skin.

'It doesn't matter—at least, not right now,'

he said, his mouth twisting into a grim line. 'What an impetuous fool I was to have taken you to bed!'

'Then why don't you do us both a favour and get out of it right now?'

She wasn't expecting him to take her at her word, but he did—pushing back the bedclothes with an impatient hand and moving away from the bed as if it were contaminated. But the impact of seeing him unselfconsciously naked as he walked across the room was utterly compelling and Amber couldn't seem to drag her gaze away. He went to stand by the window and all she could see was his magnificent physique, silhouetted against the gleaming moon and scattered stars. And all she could think about was how pale his buttocks looked against the deep tawny colour of his back. How it had felt to have the rough power of his muscular legs entwined with her own, which had felt so light and smooth in comparison.

Only he had made her feel bad about what had happened—and bad about herself. As if she were using her virginity as some kind of bargaining tool. As if she were nothing but a cold-blooded manipulator.

So why did she still want him, despite his

wounding words? Why did she want to feel his lips on her lips and his hands on her hips as he positioned himself over her, before thrusting deep inside her? Maybe she was one of those women who were only turned on by men who were cruel to them, just like her mother.

She licked her dry lips. 'Are you going now?' she croaked, because surely it would hurt less if he was gone.

He turned back to face her and at once she could see that he was aroused and, although she tried not to react, something in her face must have given away her thoughts because he gave a cold, hard smile.

'Oh, yes,' he said ruefully. 'I still want you, be in no doubt about that. Only this time I'm not going to be stupid enough to do anything about it.' Grabbing his clothes, he started pulling them on until he was standing in the now-creased suit he'd worn to the party.

'I'm going to bed,' he continued. 'I need to sleep on this and decide what needs to be done. I'll have breakfast sent up here tomorrow morning and then drive you back to London. Make sure you're ready to leave at eight.'

Amber shook her head. 'I don't want to

drive back to London with you,' she said. 'I'll get the train, like I did before.'

'It's not a subject which is open for negotiation, Amber. You and I need to talk, but not now. Not like this.'

She lay there wide-eyed after he'd gone, hugging her arms around her chest. And although she went to the bathroom to shower his scent from her skin, it wasn't so easy to erase him from her memory and her night was spent fitfully tossing and turning.

She was up and dressed early next morning, telling herself she wasn't hungry but it seemed her body had other ideas. She devoured grapefruit, eggs and toast with an appetite which was uncharacteristically hearty, before going downstairs to find Conall waiting outside for her with his car engine running.

She tried not to look at him as she climbed beside him and she kept communication brief, but he didn't object to her silence and said very little on the journey back to London. She stared out of the window and thought about yesterday and how green the lush countryside had seemed—and how today it seemed like a once-bright balloon from which all the air had escaped.

He drove her straight to her apartment and as he turned off the engine she couldn't resist a swipe.

'Here we are—home at last,' she said with bright sarcasm. 'Though not for much longer, of course, because soon my big, bad landlord will be kicking me out onto the streets.'

'That's what I want to talk to you about,' he said, pushing open his door.

'You're not planning on coming in?'

'No, not planning,' he said grimly. 'I *am* coming in. And there's no need to look so horrified, Amber—I'm not going to jump on you the moment we get inside.'

Oddly enough, his assurance provided Amber with little comfort. Was it possible that one episode of sex had been enough to kill his desire for her for ever? Because the man who had been so hot and hungry for her last night was deliberately keeping his distance from her this morning.

She waited until they were inside and then she turned to him, noticing the dark shadows around his eyes. As if he had slept as badly as her. 'So. What's the verdict?'

His mouth was unsmiling and his voice was heavy. 'I think we should get married.'

Amber blinked in astonishment and, even though she knew it was *insane*, she couldn't quite suppress the flicker of hope which had started dancing at the edges of her heart. She pictured clouds of confetti and a lacy dress, and a rugged face bending down to kiss her. She swallowed. 'You do?'

'Yes.' Navy eyes narrowed. 'I know it's far from ideal but it seems the only sensible solution.'

'I think I need to sit down,' said Amber faintly, sinking onto one of the white leather sofas beneath the penetrating brilliance of his gaze. And now that her heart had stopped pounding with a hope she realised was stupid, she tried to claw back a little dignity. 'Whatever gave you that idea that I would want to marry you?'

His gaze burned into her. 'Didn't it enter your mind for a moment that giving me your virginity would trouble my conscience? I feel a responsibility towards you—'

'Then don't—'

'You don't understand,' he interrupted savagely. 'I have betrayed the trust of your father by taking advantage of you.' His voice hardened. 'And trust is a very big deal to me.'

'He won't know. Nobody will know.'

'*I* will know,' he said grimly. 'And the only way I can see of legitimising what has just happened is to make you my temporary wife.'

She stared at him defiantly. 'So you want to marry me just to make yourself feel better?'

'Not entirely. It would have certain advantages for you, too.'

She opened her mouth and knew she shouldn't say what she was about to say—but *why not*? He'd seen her naked, hadn't he? He'd been deep inside her body in a way that nobody else had ever been. He'd heard her cry out her pleasure with that broken kind of joy as she'd wrapped her legs around his back. What did she have to lose? 'What, like sex?'

But he shook his head, his hair glinting blue-black in the watery spring sunshine. 'No,' he said. 'Most emphatically not sex. I don't want the complications of that. This will purely be a marriage of convenience—a short-lived affair with a planned ending.'

She screwed up her eyes, trying not to react. One brief sexual encounter and already he'd had enough of her? 'I don't understand,' she said, desperately trying to hide the hurt she felt at his rejection.

He walked over to the window and stared out at the view for a moment before turning back to face her. 'Your father wanted you to stand on your own two feet—and as a wealthy divorcee you'll be able to do exactly that.'

'A wealthy divorcee?' she echoed hoarsely.

'Sure. What else did you think would happen—that twenty-five years down the line we'd be toasting each other with champagne and playing with the grandkids?' He gave a cynical smile. 'We'll get married straight away—because a whirlwind marriage always makes a gullible world think it's high romance.'

'But you don't, I suppose?'

His mouth hardened. 'I'm a realist, Amber—not a romantic.'

'Me, too,' she lied.

'Well, that makes it a whole lot easier, doesn't it? And you know what they say... marry in haste, repent at leisure. Only nowadays there's no need to do that. We'll split after three months and nobody will be a bit surprised. I'll settle this apartment on you and agree to some sort of maintenance. And if you want my advice, you should use the opportunity to go off and do something useful with your life—not go back to your former, worthless existence. Your father will see you blossom and flourish with your new-found independence. He's hardly in a position to berate you for a failed marriage—and my conscience will be clear.'

'You've got it all worked out, haven't you?' she said slowly.

'I deal in solutions.' His gaze drifted to her face. 'What do you say, Amber?'

She looked away, noticing a red wine stain on the white leather of the sofa as he waited for her answer. The trouble was that on some level she wasn't averse to marrying him and she wasn't quite sure why. Was it because she felt safe and protected whenever he was around? Or because she was hoping he'd change his mind about the no-sex part? Surely a virile man like Conall wouldn't be prepared to co-exist platonically with a woman—no matter how fake or how short their relationship was intended to be.

And look what he was offering in return. At least as a divorcee she would have a certain respectability. A badge of honour that someone had once wanted her enough to marry her…

Except that he didn't. Not really. He didn't love her and he didn't want her.

That old familiar feeling of panic flooded through her. It felt just like that time when she'd been shipped off to her dad's after her mother had died. He hadn't wanted her, either, not really—and neither did Conall. It was a grim proposition to have to face until she considered the alternative. No money. No qualifications. No control. She swallowed. In an ideal world she would turn around and walk out, but where would she go?

Couldn't this marriage be a stepping stone to some kind of better future?

'Yeah, I'll marry you,' she said casually.

CHAPTER NINE

IT WASN'T A real wedding—so no way was it going to feel like one.

It was a line Amber kept repeating—telling herself if she said it often enough, then sooner or later she'd start believing it. Her marriage was nothing but a farce. A solution to ease Conall's conscience and set her up financially for the future. This way, nobody would have to lose face. Not her and not Conall.

But weddings had a sneaky knack of pressing all the wrong buttons, no matter how much you tried not to let them. Despite the example set by both her parents, Amber found herself having to dampen down instincts which came out of nowhere. Who knew she would secretly yearn for a floaty dress with a garland of flowers in her hair? Because floaty dresses and flowers were romantic, and this had nothing to do with romance—Conall had told her that and she had agreed with him. This was a transaction, pure and simple. As emotionless as any deal her Irish fiancé might cut in the boardroom.

So she opted for a dress she thought would be *suitable* for the civil ceremony—a sleek knee-length outfit by a well-known designer, with her hair worn in a heavy chignon and a minimalist bouquet of stark, arum lilies.

The ceremony was small. Her father, still in his ashram, had not been able to attend—and Conall had insisted on keeping the celebrations short and muted.

'I don't want this to turn into some kind of rent-a-crowd,' he'd growled. 'Inviting a bunch of my friends to meet a woman who isn't going to be part of my life for longer than a few weeks is a waste of everyone's time. As long as we give the press the pictures they want, nobody will care.'

But on some level *Amber* had cared. She tried to convince herself that it was a relief not to have to invite anyone and have to maintain the farce of being a blissfully happy bride. She told herself that she was perfectly cool with the miniskirted Serena and another of Conall's glamorous assistants being their only two witnesses on the day.

But hadn't some stupid part of her *wanted* Conall to take her into his arms when he'd slipped the thin gold band on her finger—and to kiss her with all the passion he'd displayed on that moonlit night in his country house? He hadn't, of course. He had waited until they got outside, where a bank of tipped-off photographers was assembled, and it was only then that he had kissed her. From the outside it must have looked quite something, for he held her close and bent over her in a masterful way which made her heart punch out such a frantic beat that for a minute she felt quite dizzy. But his lips had remained as cold and as unmoving as if they'd been made from marble—and it didn't seem to matter what she said or did, she couldn't remember seeing him smile.

They had taken the honeymoon suite at the Granchester Hotel, even though Conall had an enormous house in Notting Hill, which Amber had visited just twice before. But both occasions had felt dry and rather formal and she'd felt completely overwhelmed by the decidedly masculine elements of his elegant town house.

'I think it's best if we stay on neutral territory for the first few days.' His words had been careful. 'It lets the world know we're man and wife, but it will also allow us to work out some workable form of compromise as to how this…*marriage* is going to work.' He'd paused and his midnight-blue eyes had glinted. 'Plus the hotel is used to dealing with the press.'

The hotel seemed used to dealing with pretty much everything. Their suite was huge, with a dining room laid up to serve them a post-wedding meal, a vast sitting room, and a hot tub on the private and very sheltered rooftop garden. Rather distractingly, the king-sized bed had been liberally scattered with scarlet rose petals—something which had made Conall's mouth harden as he'd walked into the bedroom, while pulling loose his tie.

'Why the hell do they *do* that?' he asked.

Amber paused in the act of removing the pins from her hair, relieved to be able to shake it free after the tensions of the long day, even though a feeling of apprehension about the night ahead was building up inside her. 'Presumably they like to think they're adding to the general air of romance.'

'It's so damned corny.'

Kicking off her cream shoes, Amber sank down on one of the chairs and looked at him, a trace of defiance creasing her brow. 'So now what?'

It was a question Conall had been dreading and one he still hadn't quite worked out how to answer, despite it looming large in his thoughts during the days since she'd agreed to marry him, while they'd waited for the necessary paperwork to go through. Hadn't he thought she might phone him up and tell him she'd changed her mind? That she'd tell him it was insane in this day and age for two people to go through with a marriage neither wanted, just because they'd had casual sex and she had been a virgin?

There had been a big part of him which had *wanted* her to do that. Because whichever way you looked at it, he was now trapped with her for the next three months. Their relationship had to look real, which meant he'd have to be with her—as a new husband would be expected to be with his wife. And he didn't *do* sustained proximity. He liked his freedom and the ability to come and go. He always demanded an escape route and a get-out clause whenever he was in a relationship. And this *wasn't* a relationship, he reminded himself grimly.

He walked over to the ice bucket, which was sitting next to two crystal flutes and yet more scarlet roses, and pulled out a bottle of vintage champagne.

'I think we deserve a drink, don't you?' he said, glancing over at her as he popped the cork.

'Please.'

Trying hard to avert his gaze from the splayed coltishness of her long legs, he handed her a glass. 'Here.'

Amber took the glass and studied the fizzing golden bubbles for a moment before looking up into his eyes. 'So what shall we drink to, Conall?'

He sat down opposite, deliberately settling himself as far away from her as possible. What he would *like* to drink to wasn't a request for long life or happiness. No. What he needed right then was to be granted some sort of immunity. A sure-fire way to stop thinking about her sensuality—a sensuality which seemed even more potent now that he'd sampled her delicious body for himself. He wondered how it was possible for a woman to be so damned sexy when she'd only ever had sex once before.

He felt his throat thicken, but he had vowed that he was going to forget that night and put it out of his mind. To push away the ever-creeping temptation to do it to her all over again... and again. He swallowed as he felt the hard throb of desire at his groin and the sudden distracting thunder of his pulse. 'To an argument-free three months?'

She raised her eyebrows. 'You think that's possible?'

'I think anything is possible, if we put our minds to it.'

'Okay. Then—purely on the subject of logistics—I'd like to know how this arrangement is supposed to work when there's only one bed?'

Sipping his champagne, he fixed her with a steady look. 'In case you hadn't noticed, it's a very big bed.'

'And you won't be...'

'Won't be what?'

'I don't know.' She shrugged. 'Tempted?'

'To leap on you?' He gave a short laugh. 'Oh, I'm one hundred per cent certain I'll be tempted because you are an extremely beautiful woman and you blew my mind the other night. But I can resist anything when I put my mind to it, Amber. Even you.'

She put the glass down on the table and tucked her legs up neatly beneath her. It was a demure enough pose—but that didn't stop his body jerking in response, nor prevent the sudden urgent desire to slide his fingers all the way up her silken thighs and to feel if she was wet for him. Was that why a sudden brief look burned between them and why she suddenly started shifting awkwardly on the chair, as if a colony of ants had crawled into her panties?

'Well, we're going to have to do *something* to pass the time.' She glanced around. 'And I haven't noticed any board games.'

'I don't think you'll find board games are the activity of choice in a world-famous honeymoon suite,' he said drily.

'So we might as well find out more about each other. A sort of getting-to-know-you session.' She fixed him with a bright smile. 'It'll come in useful if ever we're forced to compete on one of those terrible *Mr and Mrs* TV shows, before we get our divorce finalised. I've told you plenty of stuff about me but you're still one great big mystery, aren't you, Conall?'

And that was the way he liked it. Conall

drank some more champagne. Being enigmatic was a lifestyle choice. Keep people away
and they couldn't get close enough to cause
you pain. Because pain meant you couldn't
think straight. It made you lash out and lose
control. He'd lost control once—big time—
and it had scared the hell out of him. It had almost ruined his life and he had vowed it would
never happen again.

*But you lost control with Amber the other
night, didn't you? You had sex with her even
though you'd told yourself it wasn't going to
happen. You plunged deep into her body even
though your head was screaming at you to
withdraw. And you couldn't. You were like a
fly caught in her sticky web.*

Briefly, he closed his eyes. The way she'd
made him feel had been like nothing else he'd
ever experienced—as if he'd been teetering on
the brink of some dark abyss, about to dive
straight in. If he'd had his way, he would have
walked away and never seen her again.

But Amber was his wife now and that
changed all the rules. He was with her for the
duration and there wasn't a damned thing he
could do about it. And they were holed up in
this hotel with a self-imposed sex ban. What

else were they going to do but talk? Surely he needed something to occupy his thoughts other than how much he'd like to rip that damned white dress from her body. He could always have her sign a confidentiality agreement when the time came to settle the divorce. And in the meantime, wasn't there something *liberating* about for once not having to hide behind the barriers he had erected to stop women from getting too close?

'So what do you want to know about me?' he drawled. 'Let me guess. Why I've never married before? That's usually the number-one question of choice for women.'

'Why are you so cynical, Conall?'

'Maybe life has made me that way,' he said mockingly. 'Is it cynical to state the truth?'

Their gazes clashed. He thought her narrowed eyes looked like bright slithers of green glass in her pale face.

'How come you and my father are so close?'

'I told you. I used to work for him a long time ago.'

'But that doesn't explain the connection between you.' She ran her fingertip around the rim of her champagne glass before shooting him another glance. 'A connection which was intimate enough for him to ask you to take charge of my life. Why does he trust you so much, when there are very few people he does trust?'

Conall's mouth hardened. 'Because once he did me a big favour and I owe him.'

'What kind of favour?'

Putting his glass down, he leaned back in the chair and cushioned his head on his clasped hands. 'It's a long story.'

'I like long stories.'

Conall let his gaze drift over her. Maybe it was better to revisit the uncomfortable landscape of the past, than to sit here uncomfortably thinking about what a beautiful bride she made. 'It started when I won a scholarship to your brother's school,' he said. 'Did you know that?'

She shook her head.

'A full scholarship which enabled the illegitimate son of an Irish housekeeper to attend one of the finest schools in the country. It's where I learnt to ride and to shoot.' He gave a short laugh. 'To behave like a true English gentleman.'

'Except you aren't, are you?' she said slowly. 'Not really.'

He met her faintly mocking gaze. 'No, you're right. I'm not. But you have two choices when you go to a place like that—either you try to blend in and mimic all the other boys around you, or you attempt to stay the person you already are. It was because my mother had been so strict about making me study that I was there in the first place and so I vowed to stay true to my roots. I was determined she would never think I was rejecting her values.' There was silence for a moment. Up here in the totally soundproof hotel suite, he thought that the rest of the world seemed a long way away. 'And I think Ambrose admired that quality. I'd actually met him before I won the scholarship, and became friends with his son. I'd polished the windscreen of his car a couple of times, because my mother worked as house-keeper for some of his friends. The Cadogans.'

She nodded. 'I know the Cadogans.'

'Of course you do. Everyone does. They're one of the most well-connected families in England.' He heard his voice become rough, as if someone had just attacked it with coarse sandpaper. And suddenly it stopped being just a memory. It came back to him and hit him, like an unexpected wave sneaking up behind you and knocking you off your feet. He could feel his heart pounding heavily. His skin felt heated and he wanted suddenly to escape. He wanted to get out of that damned suite and start walking. Or walk right over to the chair where she sat and haul her into his arms.

'You were saying?'

Her cool prompt made the mists clear and he was tempted to tell her that he'd changed his mind and it was none of her business. But he had bottled this up for more years than he cared to remember and mightn't it be therapeutic to let it out and for Amber to see her father in a good light for once? He cleared his throat. 'My mother had worked for the family ever since she'd got off the ferry from Rosslare. They worked her long and hard but she never complained—she was grateful that they'd allowed her to bring her baby into the house.' He raised his eyebrows. 'I guess it's unusual for you to hear it this way round. To hear what life is like *below stairs*?'

'Being rich is no guarantee of happiness,' she said flatly. 'I thought that was one thing you and I agreed on. And please don't stop your story just when it was getting interesting.'

'Interesting? That wouldn't have been

my word of choice.' His mouth twisted. He thought that there were some memories which never lost their power to wound...was it any wonder he'd buried it so deeply? 'One day a diamond ring went missing—which just happened to be a priceless family heirloom—and my mother was accused of stealing it by one of the Cadogan daughters.' His heart twisted as he remembered his mother's voice when she'd phoned him and the way she'd tried to disguise her shuddering sobs. Because in all the years of heartbreak—those times when she'd waited vainly for a letter or a card from her family in Ireland—he had never once heard her cry. 'My mother was as honest as the day was long. She couldn't believe she was being labelled a thief by a family whose house she had worked in for all those years. A family she thought trusted her.' There it was again. Trust. That word which didn't mean a damned thing.

A clock chimed in one of the suite's adjoining rooms.

'What happened?' Amber asked as the chimes died away.

He gave a heavy sigh. 'In view of her long service record they decided not to press charges but they sacked her and eventually she found a job as a cleaner in a big girls' school. But she never got over it.' He felt the lump which rose in his throat. The sense of helplessness. Even now. 'She died months later—years before her time.'

'Oh, Conall.'

But he held up his hand in an imperious gesture because he didn't need Amber Carter's pity, or for her to soften her voice like that. He didn't want token *kindness*. 'That might have been the end of it if I hadn't gone back to the house and got one of the daughters to talk to me, to find out what had really happened.'

There was a pause and he noticed she didn't prompt him to continue—maybe if she had he would have stopped—but when he started speaking again he could hear the shakiness in his own voice.

'She told me that the ring had been stolen by her sister's boyfriend—a boy high on drugs and keen to purchase more. It was all hushed up, of course. My mother had simply been the scapegoat.' He gave a bitter laugh. 'So I took it on myself to exact some sort of revenge.'

'Oh, Conall,' she whispered. 'What did you do?'

'Don't look so fearful, Amber. I didn't hurt

anyone, if that's what you're thinking—but I hurt them where I knew it would matter. One night, under the cover of darkness, I took a spray can and let rip—covering their beautiful stately house with graffiti which was designed to let the world know just how corrupt they were. I caused a lot of damage to the place and they called the police. It was my word against theirs. They were one of the oldest and most respectable families in the country while I was just...' he shrugged '...a thug with a motive.'

She was silent for a moment. 'And where did my father come in?' she asked eventually.

Conall stared straight ahead, remembering the stench of unwashed bodies and the sound of voices shouting in the adjoining cells. His own cell had been small and windowless and he'd seen a glimpse of a different path which had lain before him—a path he hadn't wanted to take.

'When I was sitting in the detention centre,' he said slowly, 'with my offer of a place at university having been withdrawn and looking at the possibility of a jail term—Ambrose arrived, and vouched for me. Rafe must have called him. He said I'd been a friend of his son's for many years and that this was a one-off deviation. I don't know if he spoke to the Cadogans but all the charges against me were dropped and he offered me a job in his construction company—at the very bottom rung of the ladder. He told me I needed to prove myself and he never wanted to hear of me wasting my time and my education again. So I worked my way up—determined not to abuse his faith in me. I learnt the building trade from the inside out. I worked every hour that God sent and saved every penny I had, until I could buy my first property. And the rest, as they say, is history.'

Amber understood a lot more about Conall Devlin now—and much of it she admired. But not all. He was hard-working and loyal, but he was also heartless. But at least now she could understand some of his prejudice towards her. *Of course* he would despise someone who represented everything he most deplored. To him she was just another of those spoilt and privileged people who stamped their way through life, not caring who they trod on—just as the Cadogans had done to his mother.

She could see the pain on his face even though he was doing his best to hide it—but hiding pain was something she recognised very well. And despite everything—despite this whole crazy, mixed-up situation—all she wanted was to go up to him and put her arms around him. Sitting there in his wedding suit with his tie pulled loose and his dark hair all ruffled, he looked more approachable than she'd ever seen him and she felt a great wave of emotion welling up inside her. In that moment she hated the Cadogans and what they had done to his mother and she found herself silently applauding the graffiti. The most natural thing in the world would be to go over there and kiss him. To comfort him with her body, which was crying out to be touched by him. But sex was off the menu. He'd told her that.

She glanced at the ornate archway which led through to the bedroom and the vast, petal-strewn bed and wondered how she was going to be able to get through the night—any night—when she was forbidden to touch him. And she wanted to touch him. She wanted to feel those expert fingers caressing her and to rediscover the pleasures of sex. Should she *accidentally* roll up against him during the night, or pretend she was having a nightmare?

She drank another mouthful of champagne. No. She sensed that she would get nothing from Conall if she was anything other than truthful. He was already furious because she'd kept her virginity a secret—if she started to play games with him now he would have zero respect for her. She could spend the next three months tiptoeing round him while the tension between them grew, or she could do the liberated thing of reaching out for what she most wanted. And what did she have to lose?

'Conall?'

'No more questions, Amber,' he warned impatiently. 'I'm done with talking about it.'

'I wasn't going to ask you any more questions about the past. I was wondering more how we're going to spend this short-lived marriage of ours.' She lifted her shoulders in a shrug, suddenly aware of the softness of her body beneath the heavy material of her wedding dress. And that Conall's dark blue gaze seemed fascinated by the movement. Any movement she made, come to think of it. Should that give her the courage to carry on? 'Because despite what I said earlier, we can't talk all the time, can we? We've already done the past and we both know there isn't going to be any future.'

'You sound like someone asking a question

who has already decided what the answer is going to be.'

'Maybe I have.' She hesitated. 'All you have to do is agree with me.'

Their eyes met.

'Agree with *what*, Amber?'

'I'd like…' She licked her lips. 'What I'd really like—is for you to teach me everything you know about sex.'

CHAPTER TEN

FOR A MOMENT Conall thought he must have misheard her because it sounded like one of those fantasies men sometimes had about women. Teach her everything he knew about sex? His mouth hardened. So that she could claw her manicured nails deeper into his flesh and learn more about him than she already did?

'Why, Amber?' he questioned, trying to ignore the sudden flare of heat in his blood.

'Isn't it obvious? Because I know so little and you know so much.' She seemed to be struggling to find the right words, which he guessed wasn't surprising in the circumstances. 'And I...'

'Oh, please, don't stop now,' he said silkily. 'This is just starting to get interesting.'

She wriggled her shoulders again and Conall got a sudden disturbing flashback of how she'd looked when she'd been naked in bed, those green eyes all wide and hungry just before he'd entered her. Another fierce hit of blood made an erection jerk beneath his suit trousers.

'I know this arrangement between us isn't meant to last, but—'

'Let me guess?' he interrupted. 'One day your knight in shining armour is going to come galloping over the horizon and carry you away, and in the meantime you'd like to learn how best to turn him on?'

A little angrily, she pushed a fallen lock of hair away from her face.

'That wasn't what I was going to say. I told you. I'm not crazy about men but I've realised that I like sex. At least, I don't have very much experience to base it on, but I certainly like the sex I had with you. And it seems a pity not to capitalise on that, don't you think?'

Her cheeks suddenly went pink and, in the silence which followed, Conall could hear the shallow sound of his own breathing.

'You want to treat me like some kind of stud?'

'That's a little defensive, Conall. Couldn't

we describe it as making the most of your expertise?'

'And this would be sex without strings?'

'Naturally.'

'With no boundaries?'

'That would depend on the boundaries.'

Conall laughed. This was getting more and more like a fantasy by the minute. Gorgeous, defiant Amber asking him to teach her everything he knew about sex—with no strings?

'So what would you say if I asked you to strip for me right now?'

'I'd say that I have no experience of stripping and would be prepared to give it a try, but…'

He raised his eyebrows as he saw a trace of insecurity cross her features. 'But?'

'I want sex,' she whispered, 'but I don't want you to make me feel like an object.'

And that whispered little appeal somehow pierced his conscience and made him realise he was behaving like a boor.

'Is that what I was doing?' he said softly.

'Yes.'

He stood up and walked over to her. 'Then I guess I'd better wipe the slate clean and start all over again. Come here and let me see what I can do.'

Amber felt herself melting as he pulled her to her feet and took her face between his hands, before bending to place his lips on hers. She told herself she must be true to her words and not read anything into it, but it wasn't easy. Not when he kept brushing his lips over hers like that, as if he had all the time in the world—teasing her and tormenting her so that she felt like a cat having a cotton reel dangled before its eyes. As he skimmed his palms down over her dress she could feel the instant response of her body.

'Want to take a shower?' he murmured.

'I guess,' she said unsteadily.

He took her by the hand and led her to the giant bathroom which had an enormous wet room attached. Amber was trying to stop herself from trembling because, after having been so upfront about expressing her needs, she could hardly turn round and tell him she was having second thoughts, could she?

Because she was. Suddenly she was scared. She realised that she was going to get exactly what she had asked for—and no more. No matter how good this felt, or how much it mimicked tenderness—she needed to remember that it meant nothing. *So just enjoy it for what it is*, she told herself fiercely. *Don't demand more than he will ever give you.*

The tiled floor felt cool beneath her bare feet and he was tilting up her chin, so that their eyes were on a collision course, and it gave her a thrill of pleasure to read the raw blaze of hunger in his gaze.

'I don't know the protocol for removing a wedding dress,' he said. 'Are there all kinds of hidden panels?'

'Nope.' She gave the familiar Amber smile as she slid down the zip and stepped out of the gown. The easy, confident smile which had always hidden a multiplicity of insecurities. 'It's all me.'

It was gratifying to see his boggle-eyed look in response to what lay beneath, and maybe on some subliminal level Amber had been hoping for this outcome all along. Last time she'd undressed in front of him she had been wearing her plain bra and those hideous big knickers—which she had now replaced with some of the most provocative lingerie she'd been able to find.

Something blue was what brides traditionally wore and she had chosen a shade of blue for her underwear—the same sapphire hue as his shuttered eyes. Wisps of silk and gossamer-fine lace pushed her breasts together so that they appeared to be spilling out of the bra like ice cream piled high on twin cones. The tiny high-cut panties barely covered her bottom and he gave a small groan of appreciation as he splayed his fingers possessively over the silky triangle at the front.

'Wow. X-rated stuff,' he said softly before peeling them off and unclipping her bra. 'And the kind of lingerie I always imagined you wearing.'

'You did a lot of that, did you?' She tipped her head to one side as he stared at her breasts. 'Thinking about me in my underwear?'

'I refuse to answer that question, on the grounds it might incriminate me. And I think you'd better learn to undress me, Amber. I think my hands are shaking too much to do it with any degree of style.'

Hers were still shaking, too, and she didn't know if he noticed but she didn't care. Because suddenly she was hungry for him. Hungry to feel his hands on her skin again and that slow burst of pleasure as he pushed deep inside her.

She eased the jacket from his shoulders and laid it on a nearby stool. Next came his shirt and she freed each stubborn button until at last she could let it flutter free. She turned her attention to his belt and then slid the zip of his trousers slowly down. She gave an instinctive murmur of delight as he sprang free, hard and proud against the palm of her hand, and, even though this was a totally new experience for her, she told herself not to be shy. *Every woman has to learn some time*, she thought— and suddenly she was grateful to be learning from someone as magnificent as Conall. Experimentally, she trickled a finger down over the stiff shaft but the steely clamp of his fingers around her wrist and the stern look on his face halted her.

'No,' he said. 'To touch a man when he is as aroused as this will make me come all over your fingers and will delay the gratification you are seeking.'

Amber wanted to disagree with him. She wanted to tell him that it would delight her to see him at the mercy of her touch. And she wanted to tell him not to be so anatomical about it all—to protest that surely sex was about more than just physical *gratification*.

But she didn't say a word and not just because she didn't have the experience to back up her claim or because his words were so *graphic*. Because he was sliding on a condom and turning on the shower and hot water was gushing freely down into the wet room as he pushed her beneath the jets.

Sweet sensation flooded over her as his arms wrapped around her and he stepped in beside her. She was aware of the hot water gushing over her and the slippery feel of Conall's hair-roughened skin as he drew her closer. His dark head was bent and he closed his lips down over one nipple to suck greedily on the hardened tip. She gasped as his fingers slid between her legs and she couldn't tell whether the warmth which flooded through her came from the shower or from inside her own body. Her head fell back as he thrummed her there insistently, the urgent rhythm building relentlessly inside her.

He had made her come once before when he had been deep inside her—but the sensation of this second orgasm took her by surprise because it happened so quickly. One minute she was revelling in him touching her and the next she was gasping out her pleasure as violent spasms racked through her body. She was still gasping when he wrapped her legs around his hips and eased himself inside her, and she clamped her hands on his shoulders as he levered her back against the tiled wall and drove into her.

He was so big. A slow moan escaped from her lips. So very big. As if he had been made to fit inside her like that. As if her own body had been designed to accommodate him and only him. She could feel the heat building again and she sensed his own sudden restraint, as if he had felt it, too—so that when the spasms exploded deep inside her again, she heard him expel a deep and ragged breath. She felt his own jerking movements and heard him groan and she was completely overcome by the sensation of what was happening to her. She must have been. Why else, when her head flopped helplessly onto his shoulder, should she have the salty taste of tears on her lips?

Her eyes were closed as he turned the shower off and wrapped her in a towel, patting her completely dry before carrying her into the bedroom. He set her down on the floor while, with an impatient hand, he yanked off the bedcover so that all the red rose petals scattered down onto the beautiful Persian rug. Like giant spills of blood, she thought, with a sudden clench of her heart, as he put her into bed and climbed in next to her.

'My hair is going to go crazy if I don't brush it,' she murmured.

'Do you want to brush it?' His lips skated over her neck and his words were muffled as he murmured against her skin. 'Or could you think of something else you'd rather do?'

Her head tipped back to accommodate his lips and her eyes closed. There was really no contest. 'Something else.'

It took longer this time. As if it were happening in slow motion. His fingertips seemed determined to acquaint themselves with every centimetre of skin. His kisses were lazy and his thrusts were deep, and her orgasm seemed to go on and on for ever. Afterwards he held her trembling body very tightly and lay there, just stroking her still-damp hair, while her cheek rested against his chest and she listened to the muffled thunder of his heartbeat.

Her eyes felt heavy and her limbs seemed to be weighed with lead. Just keeping her eyes open felt like the biggest effort in the world but there was something she needed to know, and through fluttering lashes she tipped her head back to look at him.

'Conall?' she said.

'Mmm?'

She hesitated. 'You thought I'd want to know why you'd never married before and seemed surprised when I didn't pursue it.'

'And?'

'I'm pursuing it now.' Her gaze was steady. 'Why not?'

Conall took his hand away from her head, wondering why she had reacted in such a dull and predictable way and so comprehensively ruined the soft mood which had settled over him. Give a woman a little intimacy and she tried to take everything. But maybe this would be the ideal time to drive home his fundamental principles, despite the fact that he'd just enjoyed the most mind-blowing sex. He shook his head in slight disbelief. For someone who was so inexperienced, she was so *hot*. When he touched her he felt a fierce and elemental hunger he had trouble reining in. But Amber needn't know that. He felt the beat of a pulse at his temple. Amber *mustn't* know that.

'I'm surprised that someone with your history should ask that,' he drawled. 'For me, it always seemed like backing a horse with an injured leg.'

'So that's the only reason? Because the odds are stacked against it?'

She was very persistent, he thought. 'You ask too many questions, Amber,' he said softly. 'And a man doesn't like to be interrogated straight after sex.'

She met his gaze and maybe she read something in his eyes which made her realise that his patience was wearing thin.

'Okay. Shall we have some more sex, then?' she questioned guilelessly.

Silently he applauded her lack of inhibition as he thought about some of the things he'd like to do to her. To put his head between her thighs and to taste her, just for starters. He'd like to see what she looked like on all fours, with that magnificent bottom pressed into him as he took her from behind. But he was still feeling *exposed*, from all the things he'd told her, and it was time to regain control. The sex, he decided, could wait.

'Not right now, I'm afraid.'

She sounded disappointed. 'Really?'

He pushed back the sheet and got out of bed, walking over to the wardrobe and rifling through for some of the clothes he'd unpacked before the ceremony. Pulling out a pair of jeans and a sweater, he shot her a regretful glance.

'I have some work I need to do,' he said. 'And you should sleep for a while. It's been a long day. I'll wake you up for dinner later. Would you like to go out somewhere? Or I can have the hotel reserve us a table in one of the restaurants downstairs if you prefer?'

Her body tensing beneath the duvet, Amber stared at him in confusion. Dinner was the last thing on her mind. What she wanted was for him to get in beside her and to cradle her in his arms. She wanted to drift off to sleep with him *beside* her and wake up with his black head on the pillow next to hers, so that she could lean over and kiss him and have him make love to her again. But judging by his body language as he carried his clothes towards the adjoining dressing room—that was the last thing Conall wanted.

'Can't work wait?' she questioned.

'Sorry.' He flicked her a cool look. 'It may have slipped your memory but it's my job which is paying for our stay here.'

It was a statement obviously designed to remind her that she was nothing but one of life's freeloaders, and it didn't miss its mark. Amber flinched as he turned his back on her.

She didn't know how a naked man could walk across a room looking so unbelievably in command, but somehow Conall managed it. The pale jut of his buttocks and the powerful thrust of his thighs were like poetry in motion, she thought, silently willing him to turn around and look at her. Just once.

But he closed the door behind him without a second glance.

CHAPTER ELEVEN

IT WAS LIKE playing a game of cat and mouse. A game which had no rules. But despite Amber's joking remark about boundaries, there were plenty of those.

Don't ask.

Don't expect.

And don't feel. Especially that. Don't feel anything for your enigmatic and gorgeous husband, other than desire, because he certainly won't tolerate any outward show of emotion.

But Amber was fast discovering she wasn't a switch which could be flicked on and off. She couldn't blow hot one minute and cold the next. Unlike Conall.

He had woken her up on that first evening with his hand lazily caressing her breast and, after a blissful hour between the sheets, they had gone downstairs to dine in the Granches-

ter's midnight room. Glowing lights on an in-
digo ceiling mimicked the night skies and the
exotic flowers on every table were all fiery
oranges and red. And although the hotel took
their guests' privacy seriously, someone in the
restaurant managed to capture a photo on their
cell phone, which found its way into one of
the newspapers. It was funny to look at it. Or
not, depending on your viewpoint. Conall was
leaning in to listen to something Amber was
saying and, for that frozen slice of time, it actually managed to look as if he *cared*. Which
was a lie. A falsehood. All he cared about was
projecting the right *image*. Of making what
they had look real to the outside world. But
how could it, when it wasn't real?

After five days of relative confinement and
wall-to-wall sex, the newlyweds moved into
Conall's Notting Hill house, and Amber found
herself living in a brand-new neighbourhood.
It was a tall, four-storeyed house, overlooking
a central square with a beautiful, gated garden and in any other circumstances, she might
have been overjoyed to spend time in such a
glorious environment. But she felt displaced,
surrounded by Conall's things—with nothing
of her own in situ except for her clothes. It was

his territory and he had neither the need nor the desire to modify it in any way to accommodate her. And what was the point, when she would be moving out again in three months, when their short-lived marriage was over?

'I don't know if you've thought about how you're going to spend your time while I'm at work?' he'd said, eyebrows raised in mild question—after he'd finished showing her how the extremely complicated coffee machine worked.

Amber hadn't really thought about it. The recreational shopping which used to consume her now held no appeal and she seemed to have outgrown the people she'd hung out with before. She guessed the truth was that there was only one person she wanted to spend time with and that was the man she'd married— but that was clearly a one-way street. Because Conall was an expert at compartmentalising his life—a skill which seemed beyond her. Or maybe it was because he simply didn't *have* any feelings for her, beyond those of desire and responsibility.

After wake-up sex, he left the house for work and Amber found herself resenting the fact that Serena got to see him all day, while she had to be content with the few measly hours left by the time he finally made it home. At least the May weather was warm enough for her to sit outside and she bought herself a sketch pad and took a book to read in the garden square beneath one of the lilac bushes which scented the air with its heady fragrance.

She'd been there for a couple of weeks when she received a letter from her father, forwarded by Mary-Ellen, telling her how delighted he was to hear of her marriage to Conall.

> *He's a man I've always admired. Probably the only man on the planet capable of handling you.*

And Amber could have wept, because deep down didn't she agree with her father's words? Didn't she revel in the way her new husband made her feel—like a contented, purring pussycat? Weren't the times she was able to snatch with the powerful Irishman the closest thing to heaven she'd ever known?

But Conall doesn't feel that way, she reminded herself. For him this marriage was nothing but a burden—driven by a longstanding debt to her father and an overdeveloped sense of responsibility.

She found herself thinking about the future, even though she tried not to—about what she would miss when it was all over. The sex, of course—but it was all the other things which were proving so curiously addictive. It was breakfast in bed at the weekends and waking up in the middle of the night to find yourself being kissed. It was walking around London and discovering that it seemed like an entirely different city when you were seeing it through someone else's eyes, even if you were aware that your companion would rather be somewhere else.

She made herself a cup of coffee and walked across the kitchen to stare out of the window at the quiet Notting Hill street. Last night she'd woken up as dawn was breaking and the truth had hit her like an intruder trying to break in through the basement window. The realisation had shocked and scared the life out of her—once she'd finally had the guts to admit it. That she was falling for Conall and wanted to give their relationship a real chance. To work on what they'd got and see if it had the potential to last. She wanted more of him, not less, and wouldn't she spend the rest of her life regretting it if she didn't even *try* to explore its potential?

In a frantic attempt to rewind the tape—and show him she wasn't just some vacuous airhead—she started cooking elaborate meals in the evening. Fragments of a half-finished *cordon bleu* cookery course came back to her, so that she was able to present her bemused husband with a perfect cheese soufflé or the soft meringues floating in custard which the French called *îles flottantes*.

She started reading the international section in the newspaper so she could discuss world affairs with him, over dinner. And if at times she realised she was in danger of becoming a caricature of an old-fashioned housewife, she *didn't care*. She wanted to show him that there was more to flaky Amber than the mixed-up socialite who used to fall out of nightclubs.

But if she was hoping for some dramatic kind of conversion, she hoped in vain. Her cool but sexy husband remained as emotionally distant as he had ever been. And even though she adored the powerful sexual chemistry which fizzed between them, she found herself thinking it would make a nice change to have dinner together without at least one course growing cold, while Conall carried her off to the bedroom.

She wasn't sure if she had communicated some of her restlessness, but one morning Conall paused by the doorway as he was leaving for work.

'You've been cooking a lot lately,' he said. 'I think you're due a break, don't you?'

'Is that a polite way of telling me you're fed up with my food?'

He raised his eyebrows. 'Or a roundabout way of wondering if you'd like to go out for dinner tonight?'

'Even though it's a weeknight?' She tried to clamp down the stupid Cinderella feeling which was bubbling up inside her. 'I'd love to.'

'Good.' He glanced out of the window as his driver pulled up. 'Book somewhere for eight and call the office to let them know where. I'll meet you there.'

Amber booked the table and dressed carefully for dinner, aware that she felt as bubbly and as excited as if this were a bona fide first date. She'd read a lot in the newspapers about the Clos Maggiore restaurant, known as 'London's Most Romantic'. The irony of its reputation wasn't lost on her but she'd also read that the food was superb. And she wasn't asking for *romance*—she knew he didn't do *that*. She was just asking for more of the same.

She picked out a discreetly sexy dress—a silk jersey wrap in scarlet—and she was bubbling over with excitement as she hailed a cab and directed it to Covent Garden.

But her happy and expectant mood quickly began to dissolve because he didn't turn up at eight. Nor at eight-twenty. With tight lips, Amber shook her head as the waiter offered her another glass of champagne. She'd already had one on an empty stomach and now her head was swimming. She felt a bit ridiculous sitting alone when all the other tables were occupied by people talking and laughing with each other. The rustic mirrored room was supposed to resemble a garden and somehow it managed to do just that. Just a few steps away from the world-famous market and you could find yourself sitting beneath a ceiling from which hung sprigs of thick white blossom, which looked so realistic that you almost felt you could reach up and pick one. It looked almost magical, but the feeling of dread which had started to build up inside her made Amber feel anything but magical.

Did she really think that one dinner out meant that everything was suddenly going to be perfect? As if he were suddenly going to stop keeping her locked away in her own tiny little box, which was so separate from the major part of his life. That was, if he could even be bothered to show.

Surreptitiously, she glanced at her watch, not wanting anyone to think she'd been stood up—but what if she *had*?

And then, exactly thirty-five minutes after the appointed time, there was a faint commotion at the door and Conall appeared in the flowered archway. The other diners turned to look at him as he walked over to the table and sat down, ignoring the glass of champagne which the waiter placed before him.

'You're late,' she said.

'I know I am and I'm sorry.'

'What happened?' she demanded. 'Did *Serena* keep you busy?'

He frowned. 'I'm not sure what you're trying to imply, Amber—but I'm not going to rise to it. I was on a call to Prince Luciano and I could hardly cut the negotiations short to tell him I was due at dinner.'

'But it didn't occur to you that *I* might like to be involved, seeing that I was there when you first showed him the painting?'

Conall stared at her. He could see she was angry and he knew it was partly justified, but what the hell did she expect? He hadn't planned to be late, but then—he hadn't planned for the Mardovian royal to ring him to talk about the painting. And no, he hadn't thought to involve Amber in the deal because *this was not her life and it never would be.* Soon she would be gone and their marriage nothing but a memory. Didn't she realise that the boundaries he'd imposed were in place to protect them both? *That* was why he kept an emotional distance from her, why he had never repeated those earlier confidences he had shared with her, when he'd opened up to her more than he'd ever opened up to anyone and had been left feeling raw and vulnerable. What was the point of getting close to someone when the end was already in sight? When he never got close to anyone.

Yet it was harder than he'd imagined to keep his distance from the woman he'd married, or to keep thoughts of her at bay during his working day. Hard not to remember how it felt when she was in his arms at night. The growing sense that he was in danger of losing control. His mouth twisted. Because he would never lose control. Never again.

'No, of course it didn't occur to you,' she continued, her voice shaking. 'Because I'm of no consequence to you, am I? None at all!'

Conall leaned back in his chair, his narrowed eyes wary. This marriage of theirs wasn't real, so why the hell was she making out as if it were? 'You sound a little hysterical, Amber.'

Amber went very still, feeling like a small child who had been reprimanded by a very severe teacher. And suddenly all her words were coming out in a haphazard rush. Words she'd thought often enough but never planned to say, in her determination to be the cool and casual Amber she knew she was supposed to be. 'I'm fed up with being allocated a few hours in the morning before you go to work and then just sandwiched in at night, when you can be bothered to tear yourself away from the office and your beloved Serena. Weekends are better—

but you still manage to spend a great deal of time working.'

'Will you please lower your voice?' he demanded.

'No. I will not lower my voice.' She sucked in a breath, aware that two worried-looking waiters were now hovering at the edge of the room and some of the lovey-dovey couples had gone completely quiet and were staring at them with mounting looks of horror on their faces as if registering that a full-blown row was escalating. *This is what it's like for me*, thought Amber miserably, trying not to envy all those couples their closeness and unity, but failing to do so. *This is what it's like for me. This is the reality of my marriage.*

And suddenly she realised how stupid she'd been. What was it they said? That you couldn't make a silk purse out of a sow's ear. Just as you couldn't make a real marriage out of something which had only ever been a coldly executed contract. Why even try?

Had she really thought she could endure three months of this? Of trying to *just* enjoy sex when all the time her heart was becoming more and more involved with this stubborn man and would continue to do so with every second which passed? She was a woman, for heaven's sake—not a machine! She might try but she couldn't keep her emotions locked away, even if her husband had managed to do so with such flair. *Because he doesn't have any emotions!*

She leapt to her feet and some of Conall's champagne slopped over the side of the glass as the cutlery on the table clattered. She saw the dark look of warning in his eyes but she ignored it with a sudden carelessness which felt almost *heady*.

'I'm sick of being married to a man who treats me as if I'm part of the furniture!' she flared. 'Who always puts his damned work first. Who doesn't ever want to talk about stuff. *Real* stuff. The stuff which matters. So maybe I ought to admit what's been staring me in the face right from the start. It's over, Conall. Got that? *Over for good!*'

She tried to tug the gold band from her finger but, stubbornly, it refused to budge. Picking up her handbag, she rushed straight out of the restaurant, aware of Conall saying something to the waiters as he followed, hot on her heels. She'd planned to hail a cab but she didn't have time because Conall had reached her with a few long strides and was propelling her towards his waiting car—holding her by the elbow, the way she'd sometimes seen police do in films when they were arresting someone.

'Get in the car,' he said grimly and as soon as the door was closed behind him he turned on her, his face a mask of dark fury. 'And start explaining if you would—what the *hell* was that all about?'

'What's the point in repeating it? It's the truth. You don't make enough time for me.'

'Of course I don't. Because this isn't real, Amber.' The bewilderment in his tight voice sounded genuine. 'Remember?'

'Well, if it isn't real, then we need to show the watching world that there's discord between us. We can't just break up after our supposedly *romantic* whirlwind marriage without some kind of warning. We need to show that cracks have already begun to appear in our relationship and tonight should have helped.'

There were a few seconds of disbelieving silence.

'You mean,' he said, clearly holding onto his temper only by a shred. 'You mean that the undignified little scene you created back there was all just part of some charade? That you disturbed those people's dinner in order to manufacture a spat between us?'

Wasn't it better to let him think that, rather than reveal the humiliating truth that she'd wanted to search for something deeper? That her stupid aching heart was craving the love he could never give her.

'But it's true, isn't it?' she questioned, biting her lip to stop tears spilling from her eyes. 'There are cracks. It's been cracked right from the get-go. All that stuff you said about me realising some of my talents was completely meaningless. You could have done the courtesy of having me sit in on the conference call with Prince Luciano about the Wheeler painting, but you didn't. You didn't even bother to mention the negotiations. To you I'm nothing but an invisible socialite who happens very inconveniently to turn you on.'

'Well, at least you're right about something, Amber, because you certainly turn me on,' he said grimly. 'And yes, I often find myself wishing that you didn't.'

Something dark and heavy had entered the atmosphere—like the claustrophobic feeling you got just before a thunderstorm. But he didn't say another word until the front door had slammed behind them and Amber thought he might slam his way into his study or take a drink out into the garden, or even shut himself in the spare room, but she was wrong. His gaze raked over her and she saw a flicker of something dark and unknown in the depths of his sapphire eyes.

He moved like a predator, striking without warning—reaching out for her dress and hooking both hands into the bodice. He ripped it open, the delicate material tearing as easily as if it had been made of cotton wool. Amber shivered because cold air was suddenly washing over her skin and because the expression in his eyes was making her feel...*excited* and he nodded as he looked into her face, as if he had seen in it something he recognised, something he didn't like.

'And your desire for me is just as inconvenient, isn't it, Amber?' he taunted. 'You wish you didn't want me, but you just can't help it. You want me now. You're aching for me. Wet for me.'

Her lips were parched as they made a little sound, though she didn't know what she was trying to say. She could scarcely breathe, let alone think. Excitement fizzed over her skin even though she told herself she should have been appalled when her panties suffered the same fate as her dress and fluttered redundantly to the hall floor. Appalled when he started to unfasten his trousers, struggling to ease the zip down over his straining hardness.

But she wasn't appalled.

She was relieved—for surely that was a moan of relief she gave as he eased his moist tip up against her and then thrust deep inside her. She gasped. Was it anger which made this feel so raw and so incredible as she ripped open his shirt to bare his magnificent torso? Or simply the frustration that this was the only way she could express her growing feelings for him? She could bury her teeth into the hair-roughened skin of his chest and nip at him like a small animal. And although he was giving a soft laugh of pleasure in response, she knew he wouldn't be laughing when it was over.

He didn't even kiss her and she knew better than to reach her mouth blindly towards his in silent plea. And anyway, there wasn't really time for kissing. There wasn't time for anything but a few hard and frantic thrusts. It was so wild and explosive that she gave a broken cry as her orgasm took her right under and his own cry sounded like some kind of feral moan—as if something dark had been dragged up from the depths of his soul. It was only when he withdrew from her, seconds later—quickly turning his back so she couldn't see his face—that she realised he had forgotten to use a condom.

He was breathing very heavily and it was several seconds before he had composed himself enough to turn around and stare at her and his eyes looked dark and tortured. He was shaking his head from side to side.

'That should never have happened.' His bitter words sounded as if they had been dipped in acid.

'It doesn't matter.'

'Oh, but it does, Amber. It really does.' His lips twisted. 'I can't believe I just did that. That *we* just did that. It was…it was *out of control.* I don't want to live my life like that, and I won't. This marriage was a mistake and I don't know why I fooled myself into thinking it could be anything else.'

Amber stared into his eyes and saw the contempt written there, along with a whole lot of other things she would rather not have seen.

Once before he had looked at her as if she were something which had been dragged in from the dark, and it was the same kind of look he was giving her now. But back then he hadn't known her and now he did. It was rejection in its purest form and it hurt more than anything had ever hurt.

Biting back the sob which was spiralling up inside her throat, she bent down to grab her tattered panties, before rushing upstairs towards the bedroom and slamming the door behind her.

CHAPTER TWELVE

THE END OF the marriage was played out in the papers, just as the beginning had been, and Amber found herself reading the headlines with a sense of being outside herself. As if she were some random little dot high up on the wall, looking down at the mess she'd made of her life.

And it was a mess, all right. She stared down at the photo taken of them at the Granchester on their wedding night—that false and misrepresentative photo snatched by a fellow diner—while she read the accompanying text.

Whirlwind marriage over. Golden couple split.

But it turned out to be surprisingly easy to dismantle their short-lived union. Or maybe not so surprising. Because a marriage undertaken to settle a long-term debt could never be anything other than doomed, no matter how strong the sexual chemistry between them was.

During their last conversation together, Conall had told Amber he intended being 'generous' in his settlement—but she had shaken her head.

'I don't want your charity,' she'd said, trying desperately to hold on to her equilibrium when all she'd wanted was for him to put his arms around her, and to love her.

'An admirable attitude, if a little misguided,' he'd responded coolly. 'And a waste of everyone's time if you don't accept your side of the deal.'

A waste of everyone's time? She had glared at him then, because glaring helped keep the ever-threatening tears at bay.

'I'm offering you the apartment and a monthly maintenance payment,' he'd said. 'You won't have to move.'

She told herself it was pointless to deliberately make herself homeless and so, even though she rejected his offer of monthly maintenance, she accepted the deeds of the apartment and immediately put it up for sale. She couldn't bear the thought of living in a block owned by Conall and the nightmare prospect of running into him. She would buy somewhere smaller, in a less dazzling and expensive area, and use the profit she made to support herself. She would start living within her means and take no maintenance from him. And she intended to get a job.

She sold her diamond watch—slightly taken aback by how much it was worth—and with the money raised she booked onto a short degree course in translation and interpretation at the University of Bath. It was a beautiful city and far enough away from London to know that there would be no risk of running into Conall. By a fortuitous chance there was a course starting almost immediately and Amber leapt at it eagerly. It gave her something to do. Something to replace the miserable thoughts which were whirling round in her head. She didn't want to do some boring job involving grain quotas, but surely there would be other opportunities open to her? Some which might even involve travel. But first she needed a bona fide qualification and so she moved into a rented room in a house on the outskirts of the city and began to work harder than she'd ever worked in her life.

She'd never shared a flat or lived on a reduced budget before and she soon became used to running out of milk, or eating cornflakes for lunch. She discovered that a cheap meal of pasta could taste fantastic when you shared it with three other people and a bottle of cheap wine. And if at night she found sleep eluding her and tears edging out from between her tightly closed eyes, she would hug her arms around her chest and tell herself that soon Conall Devlin would be nothing but a distant memory.

Would he?

Would she ever forget that rare smile which sometimes dazzled her? That lazy way he had of stroking her hair just after they'd made love?

Had sex, she corrected herself as she tossed and turned in the narrow bed. He'd only married her because of the debt he'd felt he owed her father. Other than that, it had really only ever been about the sex. It must have been— because when she'd told him not to bother contacting her again just before she'd left London, Conall had taken her at her word. To Amber's initial fury and then through the dull pain of acceptance, she realised he was doing exactly as she had asked him to do. He hadn't called. Not once. Not a single text or a solitary email had popped into her inbox to check how she was doing in her new life. All negotiations had been dealt with through his lawyers. And she was just going to have to learn to live with that.

June bled into July and a monumental heatwave brought the country almost to a standstill. Sales of ice cream and electric fans soared. Riverbeds dried and the grass turned a dark sepia colour. There was even talk of water rationing. One evening Amber was sitting in the dusty garden after college, when she heard the doorbell ringing loudly through the silent house. It was so hot she didn't want to move and as a rivulet of sweat trickled down her back she hoped someone else would answer it.

She could hear the distant sound of voices. A deep voice which she didn't really register because she was holding her face up, trying to find the whisper of breeze she thought she had detected on the air. And then she heard footsteps behind her and a deep voice that sent shivers racing down her spine—shivers which should have been welcome in the extreme heat, if they hadn't been underpinned by emotions far too complex to analyse.

She lifted her head slowly, telling herself not to react—but how could she possibly *not* react when she'd spent weeks thinking of him and dreaming of him? Hadn't it been an integral part of some of her wildest fantasies that he should suddenly appear in this house, like this? Greedily, her gaze ran over him. His eyes were as shuttered as they had ever been and his jaw was still shadowed blue-black. His concession to the warmer weather meant he was wearing a T-shirt with his jeans, which immediately made her start wishing it were the dead of winter, because then she wouldn't have to stare at that hard, broad torso. She wouldn't have to remember when those rippling biceps had wrapped themselves so tightly around her before carrying her off to bed.

'Conall!' Her throat felt dry and constricted. Her head felt light. 'What are you doing here?'

'No ideas?'

She shook her head. 'No.'

'Even though there's a question we both know needs answering?'

She licked her lips. 'What question is that?' she said hoarsely.

There was a pause. 'Are you carrying my baby?'

The pause which followed was even longer. 'No.'

Conall was taken aback by the shaft of regret which speared through his body and embedded itself deep in his heart. He was briefly aware of the fact that somewhere inside him a dim light had been snuffed out. He wondered how it was possible to want something more than you'd ever wanted anything, and only discover that once the possibility was gone.

He stared into Amber's pale face. At the tremble of her lips. He thought how different she looked from the woman he'd found fast asleep on that white leather sofa. Calmer. With an air of serenity about her which gave him a brief punch of pleasure. But he could see anger flickering in her grass-green eyes as she drew her shoulders back and brushed a lock of ebony hair away from her face with an impatient hand.

'Okay, you've had the answer you presumably wanted, so now you can go.'

'I'm not going anywhere.'

She narrowed her eyes. 'What I don't understand, Conall, is why you've come all this way in order to ask a question which didn't need to have been asked in person. You could have texted or emailed me. Even phoned. But you didn't.'

'It isn't about the question.'

'No? Then what is it about?'

Conall met her gaze and let her fury wash over him like a fierce tide. He had tried to stay away from her—telling himself that it was for her own good, as well as his. But something just kept drawing him back to her—and now that he was here, he felt curiously exposed. He knew she deserved nothing less than the truth, but that still didn't guarantee him the outcome he longed for. It was fork-in-the-road time, he realised. It was time to stop hiding behind the past. To reject the emotional rules he'd lived by for so long. 'I don't know if you can ever forgive me for the way I behaved on our last evening together,' he said, in a low voice.

She frowned. 'You mean…what happened in the hall?'

'Yes,' he said roughly. 'That's exactly what I mean.'

She shrugged with the expression of someone who planned to say exactly what was on their mind—and to hell with the consequences. 'We had some pretty raw and basic sex, which I thought you'd enjoyed—I certainly did, even if you completely ruined my dress and some perfectly good underwear.'

His mouth gave a flicker of a smile. 'You're missing the point, Amber.'

'Am I?' Her voice went very quiet. So quiet it was almost a whisper. 'Yet you were the one who taught me that no sex was bad sex, unless one person happened to object to it.'

'Yes, I know I did. But I lost control.' He felt a lump in his throat. 'For a moment I saw red. I felt consumed by something which seemed to consume *me*. It was as if I was powerless to stop what was happening and I didn't like that.'

'So what? Everyone loses control some time in their lives—especially after a blistering row. What's the matter, Conall—did you think you were going to run off to find a handy canister of paint and start spraying graffiti all over the walls?' She gave an impatient shake of her head. 'I don't have a degree in psychology, but I've seen enough therapists in my teenage years to realise that what you call *staying in control* means never letting any emotion out—so that when you do, it just explodes. So why not do what everyone else does and just let yourself *feel* stuff?'

Her words made sense and deep down he knew it, but did he have the courage to admit that? The courage to reach inside himself for something he'd buried for as long as he could remember? Because yes, that something was emotion. His mother had been uptight, he recognised that now—she'd allowed herself to be defined by a youthful indiscretion, so keen never to repeat it that she had locked away all her feelings and desires. And hadn't he done the same?

There had been other factors, he recognised that, too. He'd grown up in a house where he'd never fitted in. A house where his intellect and natural athleticism had made him physically and mentally superior to the men who ruled the Cadogan household—but their wealth and power had allowed them to patronise him. Amber had accused him of having a chip on his shoulder right at the beginning of their relationship—and she had been right.

But he'd learnt his lesson. Or tried to. He

had come here today with only one thing on his mind, and that thing was her.

He looked at her. 'What if I told you that I agree with every word you say?'

She narrowed her eyes suspiciously. 'And what's the catch?'

'No catch. If you can accept that I've been a fool. That I've been arrogant and stubborn and short-sighted in nearly letting the most wonderful thing which has ever happened to me slip through my fingers. And that is you. You I want. And you I miss.' His voice deepened, but there was a break in it. 'Because I love you, Amber, and I want you back.'

She shook her head, struggling a little as she got out of the deckchair. 'But you don't *do* love,' she said. 'Remember?'

'I didn't do a lot of things. If you want the truth, I didn't really live properly until I met you.' He gave a short laugh. 'Oh, don't get me wrong—to the outside world I had everything. I made more money than I knew what to do with. I ate in fine restaurants and owned amazing houses, with great works of art adorning my walls. I could travel to any place in the world and stay in the best hotels, and date pretty much any woman I wanted.'

He stopped speaking and for a few seconds he seemed to be struggling to find the right words.

'But I don't want any other woman but you because everyone pales in comparison to you, Amber,' he said, and his voice was raw. 'I thought you represented everything I didn't want—but it turns out you're everything I do. You're sharp. Irreverent. Adaptable. You make me laugh and, yes, you frustrate the hell out of me, too. But you always challenge me—and I'm the kind of man who needs a challenge. And so...'

'So?' she echoed a little breathlessly as he walked across the scorched brown grass and took her in his arms.

'We did a lot of stuff in public—*for* the public. But this is private. This is just for us. I have something I want to give you, but only if you can tell me something—and I want complete honesty from you.' He swallowed. 'And that is whether you love me back.'

Amber savoured the moment and made him wait for a few seconds—she felt almost as if it was her *duty* to do so. Because Conall had made her feel very insecure in his time and he needed to know that they shouldn't put each other through this kind of thing, ever again. But she couldn't hide the smile which had begun to bloom on her face. It spread and spread, filling her with a delight and a sunny kind of joy.

'Yes, I love you,' she said simply. 'I love you more than I can ever say, my tough and masterful Irishman.'

'Then I guess I'd better do this properly.' He glanced around, but, although the garden was deserted except for a dejected-looking starling pecking at the bare ground, they were still visible to the bedroom windows of the adjoining houses.

'Is there anywhere more private we could go?'

Breathlessly she nodded and laced her fingers in his, leading him up the rickety old stairs until they reached the tiny box room which was her bedroom. She watched his face as he looked around, seeing disbelief become admiration and then avid curiosity. He walked across the bare floorboards to the painting she was halfway through, and stared very hard at the vibrant splashes of yellow and green, edged with black.

Turning round, he looked at her. 'You've been painting,' he said.

'Yes.' Her voice was a little unsteady. 'And I have you to thank for that. I realised that you were right. That you didn't say things you didn't mean—and your praise has somehow managed to resurrect my crushed self-belief.' She smiled. 'I may never be able to sell any of these—I may not even want to. But you made me believe in myself, Conall—and that's worth more to me than anything.'

'I'm hoping this might be worth something to you, too—in purely romantic terms, rather than monetary ones,' he said gruffly as he produced a small box from the back pocket of his jeans.

And to Amber's shock he went down onto one knee as he held up a ring with an emerald at its centre—big as a green ice cube—surrounded by lots of diamonds. 'Will you marry me again, Amber? Only in a church this time. Properly. Surrounded by family and friends?'

Amber felt like a princess as she stared at the glittering ring, even though Conall had once reprimanded her for behaving like one. But this was different and she suddenly realised why. She was *his* princess and she always would be. He'd changed her in many ways, but she'd helped change him, too. He'd tamed her—a bit—and somehow she'd managed to tame him right back.

She drew in a deep breath. 'Yes, Conall, I'll marry you again today, tomorrow, next year or next week. I'll marry you any way you want, because you have given me back something I didn't realise I'd lost—and that something was myself,' she said, and now she didn't bother to hide the tears which were welling up in her eyes, because how could she berate him for not showing emotion and then do exactly the same herself? Even so, it was a couple of minutes until she had stopped crying enough to be able to speak. 'You made me realise that there was something inside the empty shell of a person I'd become,' she whispered. 'And I thank you for that from the bottom of my heart. It's one of the many reasons why I love you with every cell of my body, my darling. And why I always will.'

EPILOGUE

OUTSIDE, THE NIGHT was dark and the snow tumbled down like swirling pieces of cotton wool. Conall looked at the layer of white on the ground which was steadily growing thicker. In a few short hours it had transformed the Notting Hill garden into a winter wonderland.

'I really think…' he turned away from the window and walked over to where his wife was just finishing brushing her hair '…that we ought to think about leaving.'

Amber put the brush down and looked at him, a lazy smile on her face. 'In a minute. There's plenty of time—even with the snow. The table isn't booked until eight. Kiss me first.'

'You, Mrs Devlin, are a terror for wanting kisses.'

Her eyes danced in response. 'And you're not, I suppose?'

'I confess to being rather partial to them,' he admitted, pushing her hair away from her face and bending his head towards her, kissing her in a way which never failed to satisfy and frustrate him in equal measure. He never kissed her without wanting her and he couldn't ever imagine not wanting her. They couldn't get enough of each other in every way that mattered, and he thanked God for the day he'd walked into her life and seen her lying fast asleep amid the debris of a long-forgotten party.

His vow to marry her *properly* had remained true and deeply important to him and their wedding had taken place in a beautiful church not far from their country house. He remembered slowly turning his head to look at Amber as she walked down the aisle, his heart clenching with love and pride. She'd looked like a dream in her simple white dress, fresh flowers holding in place a long veil which floated to the ground behind her. As Conall had remarked to her quietly at the reception afterwards, if there was any woman on the planet who was qualified to wear virginal white, it was her. And when challenged on the subject by his feisty wife, he agreed that it gave him a feeling of utter contentment to know he was the only man she had ever been intimate with. And although she might have teased him about his old-fashioned attitude, deep down he knew she felt the same.

Ambrose had returned from his ashram in time for the ceremony, bronzed a deep colour, with clear eyes and looking noticeably thinner. He'd announced that he'd fallen in love with his yoga teacher and she was planning on joining him in England, just as soon as she got her visa sorted. Amber had briefly raised her eyebrows, but told Conall afterwards that she had learnt you had to live and let live, and that nobody was ever really in a position to judge anyone else. And Conall had opened up her mind to the realisation that her father wasn't all bad—he just had flaws and weaknesses like everyone else. They all did.

And families could be complicated. She knew that, but she also knew it felt better when they were together, rather than apart. She'd encouraged Conall to trace some of his mother's relatives, discovering that the world had moved on and nobody was remotely bothered by the fact that a grown man had been born not knowing who his father was. Several of his aunts were still alive and he had lots of cousins who were eager to meet him, which was one of the reasons why they'd chosen Ireland as their honeymoon destination.

Her half-brother Rafe even made it back from Australia in time for the wedding—causing something of a stir among the women present. Almost as much as the guest of honour—Prince Luc—who could be overheard telling Serena that he had played matchmaker to the happy couple.

The Prince had bought the Wheeler portrait and it now hung next to its sister painting in his Mediterranean palace and next month Conall and Amber were visiting the island of Mardovia, to see them together—at the Prince's invitation. Amber was very excited about the prospect of speaking Italian in front of her husband, very aware that it turned him on to listen to her saying stuff he simply didn't understand! Just as she was excited by the part-time art course she'd started to attend in London, where her tutor encouraged her distinctive style of painting just as much as her husband did.

But tonight they were going to Clos Maggiore—their favourite restaurant—where they'd had the furious row which had been such a flashpoint in their relationship, but where tonight they would sit happily beneath the boughs of white blossom, as contented as any of the other couples who ate there. And Amber would refuse her customary glass of pink champagne and tell Conall what she suspected he would be delighted to hear, even though it had come as something of a shock to her when she'd found out. She thought they'd been so careful…

She looked up into his shuttered eyes. Would he be a good father? A lump rose up in her throat. The very best. Just as he was the very best husband, lover and friend a woman could ever want.

'I love you, Conall Devlin,' she whispered.

His eyes crinkled into a smile—a faint question in their midnight depths. 'I love you, too, Amber Devlin.'

And suddenly she didn't want to wait until they were in the restaurant, gorgeous though it was. This was private, just for them, just like the time when he'd knelt on the bare floorboards of her tiny room in Bath and produced an emerald ring as big as a green ice cube. Feeling stupidly emotional, she tightened her arms around his neck and brushed her lips over his as the excitement grew and grew inside her. 'And this might be a good time to tell you my news...'

* * * * *

If you enjoyed this story,
check out these other great reads from
Sharon Kendrick

THE SHEIKH'S CHRISTMAS CONQUEST
CLAIMED FOR MAKAROV'S BABY
THE RUTHLESS GREEK'S RETURN
CARRYING THE GREEK'S HEIR
CHRISTMAS IN DA CONTI'S BED

Available now!

LARGER-PRINT BOOKS!
GET 2 FREE LARGER-PRINT NOVELS PLUS
2 FREE GIFTS!

◆HARLEQUIN®

Romance

From the Heart, For the Heart

YES! Please send me **The Montana Mavericks Collection** in Larger Print. This collection begins with 3 FREE books and 2 FREE gifts (gifts valued at approx. $20.00 retail) in the first shipment, along with the other first 4 books from the collection! If I do not cancel, I will receive 8 monthly shipments until I have the entire 51-book Montana Mavericks collection. I will receive 2 or 3 FREE books in each shipment and I will pay just $4.99 US/ $5.89 CDN for each of the other four books in each shipment, plus $2.99 for shipping and handling per shipment.*If I decide to keep the entire collection, I'll have paid for only 32 books, because 19 books are FREE! I understand that accepting the 3 free books and gifts places me under no obligation to buy anything. I can always return a shipment and cancel at any time. My free books and gifts are mine to keep no matter what I decide.

263 HCN 2404   463 HCN 2404

Name	(PLEASE PRINT)	
Address		Apt. #
City	State/Prov.	Zip/Postal Code

Signature (if under 18, a parent or guardian must sign)

Mail to the **Reader Service:**

IN U.S.A.: P.O. Box 1867, Buffalo, NY 14240-1867
IN CANADA: P.O. Box 609, Fort Erie, Ontario L2A 5X3

MMLPBPA15